HOME, I RE1

To David,

Thank you for all your help with ideas for my Book Cover.

Enjoy!

Kind Regards
John

HOME, I REMEMBER FOREVER

DUNSTANBURGH CASTLE

JOHN ADAMS

YOUCAXTON PUBLICATIONS
OXFORD & SHREWSBURY

Written in the Midlands & Northumberland.

Copyright © John Adams 2018

The Author asserts the moral right to
be identified as the author of this work.

ISBN 978-1-912419-10-4
Printed and bound in Great Britain.
Published by YouCaxton Publications 2018

All rights reserved. No part of this publication may be reproduced,
stored in a retrieval system, or transmitted in any form or by
any means, electronic, mechanical, photocopying, recording
or otherwise, without the prior permission of the author.

This book is sold subject to the condition that it shall not, by way of
trade or otherwise, be lent, resold, hired out or otherwise circulated
without the author's prior consent in any form of binding or cover
other than that in which it is published and without a similar condition
including this condition being imposed on the subsequent purchaser.
YouCaxton Publications
enquiries@youcaxton.co.uk

For our Christine

Contents

The Story Behind the Story   ix

Prologue:
Holy Island,
2nd January 1963

Chapter 1: The Storm	3
Chapter 2: Saint Mary's Church	5
Chapter 3: The Discovery	7
Chapter 4: The Rectory	10
Chapter 5: Deciphering the Discovery	13
Chapter 6: Awaiting News	15
Chapter 7: The Shopping Trip	17
Chapter 8: An Unscheduled Stop	22
Chapter 9: Return to Holy Island	25

Part One:
Dunstan Steads,
Early 14th Century

Chapter 10: A Young Agnes	31
Chapter 11: A Young Hugh	33
Chapter 12: The Arrest	38
Chapter 13: A Concerned Hugh	40
Chapter 14: The Gaol	43
Chapter 15: The Verdict	46

Chapter 16: A Goodbye	49
Chapter 17: Incarceration	51
Chapter 18: Avoiding Family	53
Chapter 19: Transporting the Prisoner	55
Chapter 20: A Negotiation	57
Chapter 21: The Opportunists	61
Chapter 22: A Plan Unfolds	63
Chapter 23: The Dungeons	66
Chapter 24: Prisoner for Sale	68
Chapter 25: Criggle's Advances	72
Chapter 26: The Drink	74
Chapter 27: Reacquainted	77
Chapter 28: Decision Required	79
Chapter 29: Criggle Sleeps	82
Chapter 30: Raising the Alarm	84
Chapter 31: Sugar Sands	86
Chapter 32: The Crossing	88
Chapter 33: Distant Sounds	92
Chapter 34: Seeking Revenge	94
Chapter 35: A Sad Loss	97
Chapter 36: Geeson Is Discovered	99
Chapter 37: On the Piers	101
Chapter 38: Midnight Hour	103
Chapter 39: A Race Begins	105
Chapter 40: Home, I Remember Forever	107

Part Two
London Bound

Chapter 41: Making Plans	111
Chapter 42: In Pursuit	113
Chapter 43: A Captain Contemplates	115

Chapter 44: Brief Respite	117
Chapter 45: Double Cross	120
Chapter 46: A Trap Awaits	122
Chapter 47: The Marshes	126
Chapter 48: No Show	128
Chapter 49: Rotherham Beckons	130
Chapter 50: Fall From Grace	132
Chapter 51: No More Waiting	136
Chapter 52: Aromas	138
Chapter 53: The Helper	143
Chapter 54: The Wager	147
Chapter 55: The Offer	149
Chapter 56: Meeting the Captain	152
Chapter 57: Passage Secured	154

Part Three
Portugal Bound

Chapter 58: The Isolde	159
Chapter 59: The Proposal	161
Chapter 60: Ceremony at Sea	163
Chapter 61: The Rename	166
Chapter 62: Land Approaches	169
Chapter 63: A New Aquaintance	171
Chapter 64: A New Residence	173
Chapter 65: New Addition	176
Chapter 66: The Alcove	179
Chapter 67: The Griever	182
Chapter 68: A Difficult Conversation	186
Chapter 69: The Physicker	190
Chapter 70: Left with a Friend	192
Chapter 71: The Amélia	195

Part Four
Homeward Bound

Chapter 72: At Sea Again	199
Chapter 73: The Couriers	203
Chapter 74: Familiar Territory	206
Chapter 75: A Calm Sea	209
Chapter 76: A Fallen Angel	211
Chapter 77: The Journal	214
Chapter 78: The Brothers	216
Chapter 79: Wanted Dead or Alive	218
Chapter 80: The Archer	222
Chapter 81: An Old Friend	225
Chapter 82: No Hope	229
Chapter 83: Edwyn's Suggestion	231

Part Five
Holy Island, 1963

Chapter 84: Tavira 369288	237
Chapter 85: A Distant Relative	241
Chapter 86: The Flight	243
Chapter 87: The Flying Scotsman	245
Chapter 88: Handing Over the Journal	250
Chapter 89: Castle Ruins	254
Chapter 90: The Service	256
Epilogue	259
Acknowledgements	260
Tribute to Mabel: 2016-2017	262

The Story Behind the Story

PEOPLE have asked me why did I write this novel? I guess there are several reasons. First and foremost the novel is dedicated to my partner Chrissie who once commented whilst browsing through the shelves at the wonderful bookshop Barter Books in Alnwick that there was a distinct lack of fictional books relating to her favourite castle at Dunstanburgh. I checked on the internet and found that this was indeed the case.

I have researched the family trees of both my parents with fascinating results; there are subtle elements of family history in this book. I have a fascination with the northern lights which can been seen in the county of Northumberland and they are also evident in the book.

Whilst walking along the beaches near to Greymare Rock and Dunstanburgh Castle I have often sat listening to the waves rolling in and the surf crashing onto the beach and imagined what events took place many centuries ago when the castle was inhabited.

Chrissie and I have a passion for the area and we had a bespoke commitment ring designed by local jeweller Harriet Kelsall. Inside the ring are the words in old Northumberland dialect 'Hyem I mindin on aye' which roughly translates to 'Home I remember forever', which I decided to use for my title.

I started to write the novel in my spare time. One day several months after I'd started, Harriet Kelsall rang to say that BBC Radio Newcastle's Anna Foster show was airing a programme called *Things Inspired by the North* and their researchers had found Chrissie's ring online. Here it is: https://www.hkjewellery.co.uk/ring-11627-chrissies-9ct-rose-gold-northumberland-inspired-ring. They asked if I would go live on air and discuss the ring. I was happy to do so and while I was on air I also mentioned my novel, so perhaps you were listening back then and we meet again now.

Prologue

Holy Island, 2nd January 1963

Chapter 1

The Storm

'Looks like a storm brewin', Aidan.'

'Aye, you could say that, Oswald. Look at the waves crashing over the rocks! We best get those lobster pots secured down before it arrives.'

'Ha! Don't make me laugh. There be no fishing boats going out in this weather. It's so cold, apparently Old Cyril said the sea froze over in Herne Bay Kent yesterday, an' the weather's only goin' to get worse.'

'What does he know, anyway?'

In fact, Cyril was right. The wind was relentless. Wave after wave crashed over the shoreline, depositing driftwood from miles away. The strong winds on the island left no building unscathed. The wind had also pushed the snow clouds south from Scotland and, as the blizzard raged that night, all the islanders were either inside their homes, huddled around open coal fires, or in the Crown and Anchor Public House. Inside, people were warming themselves with a pint of Alnwick brown ale or rum, revelling in the heat from the open log fire.

By eleven o'clock, the worst blizzard recorded since 1814 had gripped the island. Few people got much sleep that night, but by early morning the next day the winds had abated. Snow drifts over six feet tall had cut the island off from the mainland. It even took two Land Rovers with snow-plough attachments, deployed from the Chillingham Estate on the mainland, until Sunday 6th January to make the roads passable again.

No fishing boats went out during this time, which the fishermen used to repair their fishing nets and sandpaper down the worn paint on the fishing cobles which had been landed on sheltered areas of the beach. These fishing vessels were reliable but required yearly maintenance to ensure they could survive the violent seas off the Northumberland coast. The hulls of the boats were often painted two tone, in vibrant colours, with their registration details displayed midway along the boat.

The wicker lobster pots which lay along the harbour shoreline were either stacked more securely after the storm or repaired ready for when the boats could set sail again. A colony of seagulls flew noisily around the fisherman, hoping to find any small morsel of food. The gale proved too strong even for these seafaring birds, so they eventually retreated inland to find shelter. Many species of wildlife were suffering in this harsh winter. Those which had hibernated were in the best place. The severity of the weather had even led to reports of rare Beluga whale sightings, which normally resided in the Artic, off the Northumberland coast.

Chapter 2

Saint Mary's Church

ON this particular Sunday morning, Reverend Collins decided to walk to St Mary's the Virgin Church rather than cycle due to the perilous state of the roads – thick ice remained and a fresh sprinkle of snow had followed the work of the snow ploughs. So cold was the morning air that he felt a tightness in his chest, and as he walked clouds of visible air were expelled from his lungs. He was all too aware that the old church would not be much warmer inside.

As the reverend approached the church, he could see that the roof had been slightly damaged by the storm in the night. There had been numerous successful church roof repair appeals and, with the help of builders on the mainland, he knew the repairs would be made good in a matter of days. The reverend smiled, thinking that the good Lord himself had not spared the church from the ravages of the storm.

Entering the church, he felt the cold air rush through the door from inside. He turned on the light but the building remained in semi-darkness. The weak winter sunrise did not let much daylight through the magnificent stained-glass windows at this time of year.

As he searched for a candle to light he noticed a small amount of blood smeared across the floor. His heart started to pound faster and he could taste fear in his cold breath.

'Who would commit a crime in a holy place?', he thought to himself.

He stood frozen with fear for what felt like an age. Then a sparrowhawk flew full speed towards the reverend, narrowly missing his face, and out through the oak door into the morning light. He looked down to see feathers and a partially eaten reed warbler. Relieved to realise that he was not witnessing the aftermath of a gruesome murder, the reverend continued his search for the candles in the cold semi-darkness. For the second time that morning, his heartbeat accelerated as the voice of Marjorie, the church assistant, cut suddenly through the silence.

'Mornin' Reverend Collins, is that you?'

'Mornin' Marjorie, I'm over here. The storm has damaged the roof and cut off the power; I was just searching for some candles. I don't suppose you could help me find them?'

'Of course, Reverend Collins, they're just over here.'

Chapter 3

The Discovery

WITHIN minutes of Marjorie's arrival, the church was aglow with the light of over two dozen large candles.

Now there was a greater amount of light in the church, Reverend Collins noticed that a roof tile had impaled the wooden chancel. He looked up at the patch of blue sky that showed through amongst the wooden ceiling.

'That solves the mystery of how our feathered friends entered the church.'

'Did you say something, Reverend Collins?'

'No, Marjorie, I was just talking to myself!'

He tried to remove the tile but it was wedged firmly. As he gained extra purchase, it slowly freed itself from the wood, revealing something hidden behind it.

'Marjorie, could you please bring a candle over here? I think I've found something behind the chancel panels!'

'Yes, Reverend Collins.'

Marjorie arrived moments later and shone the candle near to where the reverend was crouched.

'What is it, Reverend?'

'It looks like a small box has been hidden behind this panel!'

'How exciting! The chancel has barely been touched since the 14th century.'

'Indeed, indeed.'

Reverend Collins placed his hand inside the damaged panel to retrieve the box-like object, and placed it on the floor near to the candle.

'What a beautiful object! What do you think it is?'

'Well, Marjorie, it's not a box – looks to me like a very old book.'

The book was skilfully made from the highest quality materials; the leather binding almost looked new and was embossed with intricate patterns. Two words were inscribed on the front.

'Look, Reverend! There's some writing, what does it say?'

'Looks like Sant? Or Saint? And the second word is Sera something?'

'Perhaps Saint Serapia?'

'Could be, Marjorie, the script is really old.'

'Here, you have a look.'

Marjorie put on her glasses.

'Umm, well, it's very difficult to make out. Could be Saint Serapia, as you said, but I couldn't be really sure.'

She carefully opened the book to reveal beautiful written words, also written in a script she did not recognise.

'It appears to be a very old form of English. What do you think, Reverend?'

'Aye, you could be right. We best put this book safely away as the morning congregation will be arriving shortly. I will contact Mrs Ford-Thomas of the Northumbrian Language Society later – she may be able to help us. It may be a significant find so I will also have to notify the Archbishop of Newcastle and perhaps also the Diocese of Hexham.'

'You really think it could be important?'

'Who knows, Marjorie, but I need to contact the Archbishop regarding the required church repairs so it is best he knows sooner rather than later.'

Chapter 4

The Rectory

ONCE the mysterious book had safely been stowed away, the morning congregation started to arrive. Reverend Collins could not fully concentrate on his sermon as his head was filled with thoughts of the book. His flock that morning was smaller than normal as this place of worship was only slightly warmer than the extreme cold outside. When the service was over, he said his goodbyes to Marjorie, put the mysterious book in his satchel and walked home to make some phone calls after lunch at the Rectory. His wife, Mrs Collins, had prepared a warm, welcoming Sunday roast beef dinner with all the trimmings and had lit a roaring log fire. Their dog Rufus, a joyful black working cocker spaniel, lay in front of it, sleeping off her morning walk.

The reverend told his wife about the events of that morning. She was also intrigued but could provide no further clues as to the origin of the book.

After lunch, Mrs Collins joined Rufus on a chair next to the log fire to read the Sunday papers while the reverend retired to his study to make his phone calls. He would call the builders and electricians regarding the church repairs the next day — they were probably in a local pub on the mainland enjoying a tipple or two.

Once he was sitting comfortably in his leather chair, the reverend made his first phone call to the Archbishop of Newcastle, hoping to get authorisation for the repairs and to discuss his discovery of the book. On the third ring, the Archbishop answered his phone.

'Good afternoon, Newcastle 2398.'

'Greetings, Archbishop, this is Reverend Collins calling from the Holy Island.'

'Hello, Reverend! I hope Mrs Collins is keep well? How may I help you?'

'Two things. First of all, the ghastly storm has caused some slight damage to St Mary's, so I'm seeking approval for its repairs, and secondly, as the chancel was damaged, I discovered a rather old book behind one of the panels. Again, I was seeking your approval to have it inspected by Mrs Ford-Thomas on the mainland. There's an inscription, possibly of some religious significance, but it's rather difficult to say. Or I could get my wife to deliver the book to you the next time she visits her family in Newcastle if you'd prefer?'

'Well, Reverend, thank you for bringing these matters to my attention. As always, I trust your judgement with regard to the repairs at St Mary's. I am sure you will deal with this expediently. As for your discovery, there is no need for Mrs Collins to trouble herself and deliver in person. Again, on this matter I trust your judgement. I agree Mrs Ford-Thomas would be the best person to help us on this matter.'

'I appreciate your faith in me, Archbishop. Should I contact the Diocese of Hexham as well?'

'No need, Reverend Collins. I am meeting him next week for an ecclesiastical gathering at Doxford Hall, so I will mention our phone conversation to him then. I would appreciate it if you could keep me updated.'

'Thank you, Archbishop, I'll be in touch. Goodbye.'

Replacing the receiver, he felt pleased that the Archbishop had trusted him to deal with the discovery of the book. He picked up the telephone again and made his second call.

'Hello, Alnwick 2269.'

'Hello Mrs Ford-Thomas, Reverend Collins calling. Sorry to trouble you, but I wonder if you could help our church with something. A book was found this morning behind a damaged panel on the chancel caused by the recent storms. It seems to be written in a very old English script, and we were hoping you could help us to decipher its contents.'

'I'm sorry to hear the church has been damaged – but not too badly I hope? It would be the dialect society's pleasure to help in any way we can. I'm visiting the island on Wednesday, so I could collect the book then if you'd like?'

'Aye, that would be splendid. Shall we say eleven o'clock at the Rectory? And Mrs Collins can provide us with morning coffee. With regards to the church damage, it was only minor and should be fixed within a few days.'

'Ok, Reverend, sounds splendid. I look forward to seeing you and your wife on Wednesday. Bye for now.'

'Bye!'

Reverend Collins replaced the receiver and wrote the appointment in his diary. The mystery would have to wait a few more days. He made a note to call the builders in the morning and then returned to his wife and Rufus for a relaxing afternoon by the fireside.

Chapter 5

Deciphering the Discovery

On Monday morning, several calls were made to the mainland tradesmen to schedule repairs for the next day. These were completed by Tuesday evening, so the church was watertight and fitted with functioning electricity once again. During the couple of days before Mrs Ford-Thomas's visit, the reverend looked through the pages of the book but could not really decipher its contents.

When Wednesday arrived, the book was placed on the middle of a desk in his study ready for inspection. His guest arrived promptly, enjoying morning coffee and homemade scones in the lounge with the Mrs Collins, while Rufus was keenly eying up any crumb spillages which she could collect later. After a general chit chat about the recent weather and family news, the three of them entered the study to look at the book. Mrs Ford-Thomas picked up the book and was silent for several minutes as she peered through some of the pages.

'Most extraordinary! Its hiding place must have protected it well – this book looks almost new. The roman numerals suggest that this book was written around the mid-fourteenth century.'

'Does it appear to be of any religious significance?'

'No, it appears to be a story about a family called Serafim-Santos. There are references to Portugal and something about a burial. May I take the book away so I can get a modern-day translation for you? It should take only a week or so if I get some of the other members of the Society to help me.'

'Yes, of course. I appreciate your help. I'll let the Archbishop know that it is in your safe keeping and perhaps of no relevance to the church.'

The book was carefully packed up and taken away for translation. The reverend made a phone call that evening to the Archbishop to keep him up to date.

The snow had begun to recede slightly and the evenings were getting lighter by a few minutes each day. Even the temperature had increased, making winter now almost bearable.

Chapter 6

Awaiting News

REVEREND Collins gladly went about his duties for the next week, patiently awaiting a phone call regarding the book. Every time the phone rang the caller could detect the disappointment in his voice once he realised it was not the one he was waiting for.

He received the call twelve days later after eating his favourite breakfast of Weetabix soaked in steaming hot milk. His wife then served him piping hot tea on the Crown Ducal Orange Tree tea set he had purchased for her as a birthday present from an antique shop in Alnwick.

The phone's shrill ring startled him. He picked up the receiver on the third ring.

'Good morning, Reverend. Sorry it has taken so long for me to get back to you, but the book took longer than I expected to decipher.'

'And what, may I ask, is your conclusion?'

'Well, basically, it's a request from a local man to be buried in the churchyard. It's quite intriguing really.'

Mrs Ford-Thomas read out the story over the phone for the next half hour while he listened attentively to every word. By the time she fell silent, the reverend had long since made up his mind.

'Yes! We must somehow try to trace the relatives of

Hugh Serafim-Santos. Thank you so much for your help. I'll be in touch.'

The Archbishop was equally intrigued and said that he would speak to the Archbishop of Westminster, who had a relative working in the Portuguese embassy there.

By mid-March the reverend was starting to think that the Archbishop had forgotten to ring London, but the phone rang one Sunday evening.

'Hello, Reverend Collins, glad I could catch you in after your service. I wanted to update you on the name search. Needless to say, unfortunately, the Portuguese embassy has offered no clues. Apparently, the name Santos Serafim is quite common – it's like Smith here in England. However, they've never heard of Serafim-Santos, so it could either be very rare or have been written down incorrectly. All I can suggest is that you ask for the book back, keep it at the Rectory for safekeeping, and should we get any more news we can take things from there.'

Disappointed, the reverend thanked the Archbishop for his help, said his goodbyes and replaced the receiver. He then called Mrs Ford-Thomas and asked her to return the book at her earliest convenience, which she did the following Tuesday. She too was disappointed by the lack of further leads. He also informed Marjorie at the following Sunday's communion.

'The Lord works in mysterious ways, Reverend. Perhaps something will crop up soon and we can solve the mystery.'

'I'm not sure I share your optimism, Marjorie, but let's hope that is the case.'

Gradually, those involved started to forget the mysterious book.

Chapter 7

The Shopping Trip

IN the July of 1963, after completing her stock take of the weekly communion wine after the Sunday service, Marjorie wrote down what she needed to purchase when she made her next shopping trip to Newcastle.

The following day was warm and sunny with not one cloud in the vivid blue sky, which was a relief after the harsh winter. Standing at the bus stop and feeling the warm summer sun on her face, she chatted with her Holy Island friends who were also travelling to Newcastle for a day's shopping. While standing there her eyes settled on the fleet of coble boats at sea which were either dropping off lobster pots or trying to catch herring which would be sent to the famous Craster Smokehouse for processing. The harsh winter had dented the incomes of the fishermen and they were keen to make up for this by working seven days a week.

The 10.18am service to Newcastle was on time and once she had paid her two shillings and sixpence return fare she sat down on the second-row seat on the Bristol diesel engine bus. This modern vehicle had comfortable seats and opening side windows, and the gentle sea breeze offered a small relief from the stifling summer heat inside. It could even travel at speeds up to forty-five miles per hour on a straight stretch of road.

As the bus pulled away a plume of diesel fumes trailed behind. The bright green painted Perryman's bus approached the crossing to the mainland; the timetable was planned around the tides as the island was cut off twice a day. Quite often, eager drivers, usually holiday makers who ignored the tidal warning signs, had their car engines flooded. In their panic, they would either have to climb into the emergency crossing hut or try to make it back to the mainland. Locals who were experienced at crossing the causeway often drove over with minutes to spare but rarely got caught out like the tourists.

On this particular day, the tide was completely out. With excellent visibility, horse riders could be seen enjoying a gallop along the flat sandy beach. In fact, with low tides one could easily walk to and from the mainland safely. Reverend Collins was walking Rufus on the beach next to the causeway; the spaniel was in her element, chasing pieces of seaweed which had been thrown for her into the shallow water.

Bamburgh Castle came into view on the left of the bus as it stopped to pick up further passengers en route. This castle was an excellent example of a well-maintained fortification; in fact, people lived there and continued to ensure that it remained in good condition. The bus continued along the coastal route and was almost half full by the time it reached Craster. Clouds of cigarette smoke lingered in the stiflingly hot bus.

Here the exquisite aroma of Craster kippers wafted through the open bus windows. Herrings had been caught and landed here for over a hundred years and these wonderfully tasting fish were a popular choice with locals and tourists alike. This traditional, family-run business used whitewood shavings and oak sawdust which was smouldering away for up to sixteen hours a day. The smoke could be seen billowing from the vents in the building which filled the air with a wonderful scent.

As the bus headed inland to join the southbound A1 to Newcastle, Marjorie caught a glimpse of Dunstanburgh Castle in the distance. This was her favourite, as it provided a breath-taking view and, no doubt, many an event had once occurred within its walls. Although it was now a ruin, there was a romantic feel to the site. During World War Two it had been identified as a potential landing site for an amphibious German invasion and, as a result, this coastal area was protected with anti-tank trenches and anti-aircraft emplacements. The pill boxes that had been constructed during the war remained here only eighteen years after the armistice. Lichens were already established on the concrete, covering a large area of the surfaces. These crusty composite organisms were mainly orange in colour and gave a rusty like appearance in the patchy areas of the surface in which they grew.

As the bus approached the great A1 just north of Alnwick it took a left turn to travel south towards Newcastle. The A1 was essentially a remnant of the Roman Empire, connecting London in England to Edinburgh in Scotland over a distance of four hundred and forty miles. The single carriageway was busy and delays of five minutes during rush hour were not uncommon. On the right-hand side of the bus, the Cheviots could be seen in this distance. These impressive hills formed a natural border between Scotland and England. They were due to arrive at Newcastle bus station a few minutes before one o'clock. However, as it approached the junction for Morpeth, a policeman standing in the carriageway ahead signalled for vehicles to slow down. Once the bus driver had come to a complete stop, he switched off the engine ignition, applied the handbrake, and slid open his window to ask the police officer what the problem was.

'Sorry, sir, but one of the Alston Coals lorries has shed its load all over the carriageway one mile ahead. The driver is ok, just a little shaken. He swerved to avoid a red deer in the road and fortunately no other vehicles are involved. You will have to divert via Ashington, though – there's no way through.'

'Aye, ok, officer, will do.'

The policeman walked away to break the bad news to the queue of four vehicles that had already built up behind the bus.

The bus driver got out of his cabin, straightening his tie in the process, and then announced to his passengers,

'Sorry, folks, you probably heard the constable — unfortunately the road is blocked ahead and the diversion I need to take will mean a late arrival at Newcastle. For those of you returning to the Holy Island please be aware that this evening's latest safe tidal crossing is at 19.02 hours. Please take this into consideration if you are returning there today.'

With this, the driver returned to his cabin, inhaling the cigarette smoke from the passengers and longing for one himself on his break. He then switched on the engine and prepared to drive off. A few of the passengers quietly grumbled but they all appreciated this was not his or the bus company's fault, but just bad luck.

Marjorie had already realised the implications of any delays in returning to the island to beat the evening tides. She thought how competent and courteous the driver was and made a mental note to write to Perryman's. She was a believer of credit where credit was due.

The bus arrived at Ashington just before noon. Concerned about the tidal crossing, Marjorie decided to disembark and make her purchases here. She thought it would also make a nice change as she had not visited the town for several years. This act of serendipity would prove to be beneficial.

Chapter 8

An Unscheduled Stop

Shortly after midday, Marjorie glanced through the leaded windows of the Broadway Wines shop as she was walking down the High Street. The shop door was painted a bright gloss claret red. She thought this would be an ideal place to purchase two bottles of wine for the church communion next week. As she opened the door a brass bell rang to alert the shop owner that a customer had entered, and the proprietor appeared from a sliding door behind the counter. He was smartly dressed in a shirt and tie and a beige smock. The tie was also claret red to match the shop door. He was probably aged around fifty and wore small, circular glasses.

'Good afternoon, Madam. How may I be of assistance?'

'I would like two bottles of red wine suitable for my local church's communion, please.'

'Certainly, Madam. Are you just visiting for the day? I haven't seen you here before.'

Marjorie explained her bus diversion as the owner walked out from behind the counter to find a suitable wine for her. She noticed that he walked with a limp. Perhaps a war injury, she thought, but she thought it may be impolite to ask.

'We have this wine just in, Madam, from Portugal. It's proving a bestseller, only two and six a bottle, and it tastes delightful.'

He handed Marjorie a bottle for her to read the label. As she read it, her face turned white. Her hands began to shake, causing the bottle to fall and smash on the tiled terracotta floor, leaving a coating of broken glass and red wine. The breaking of glass had prompted the shopkeeper's wife to enter the room.

'Are you alright, dear? Can I get you a glass of water?'

'Look at the mess I've caused! I'll pay for everything and clean it up. I'm so sorry!'

'Not to worry, dear, it's not the first time it has happened and won't be the last. Imagine if we had a parquet floor?'

With this Marjorie managed a small laugh. The shopkeeper promptly arrived with a glass of water in one hand and a mop and bucket in the other.

'You take a seat there with my wife. I'll soon clean this up.'

While the shop was being cleaned, Marjorie told his wife the story of the mysterious book. As she did this, his wife picked up another bottle and read the label.

'Serafim-Santos. Fine Wines, Algarve, Portugal.'

'I can see why you were excited. Mystery solved, perhaps? Would you like to make a telephone call to inform your church of your discovery?'

'That's very kind, thank you, but I think it's best I present the wine in person.'

The shopkeeper had heard the story while clearing up the spillage. There was little evidence of the breakage now.

'There, all done. Like new!'

'Thank you. I insist I pay for three bottles.'

'Nonsense, have these two on the house, or the shop, so to speak!'

'You are too kind. I don't suppose you have the importer's contact details?'

As he wrapped up the bottles, Marjorie passed half a crown to his wife and whispered,

'I insist.'

Once wrapped, the shop owner gave her a business card he had taken from a small wooden pine box underneath the shop counter.

'This is where I purchased the wine.'

The card read 'Mr Gary Caine, Shepherd's Bush, London, W12, Telephone London 324169.'

'Thank you so much. You have both been most kind.'

She put both of the well-wrapped bottles in her wicker shopping basket and placed the business card in her purse.

Once in the High Street again, Marjorie decided to find the nearest café, have a light lunch and try and catch the three o'clock bus home. Walking by a bright red phone box, she thought about the suggestion that the shopkeeper's wife had made regarding making a phone call. She paused for a few seconds, decided against it, and then continued on. Her discovery could wait.

As it was a glorious summer's day, she decided to sit outside Julie's Café to eat her lunch. She ordered a crab salad and a white fresh crusty roll along with a pot of fresh tea.

Having settled the bill, she walked a short distance to the nearest bus stop which was heading north. No one else was waiting in the queue. The three o'clock bus arrived promptly and on time.

Chapter 9

Return to Holy Island

The return journey back to Holy Island seemed to take an eternity, even though there were no traffic delays and few passengers were waiting at bus stops along the route. Once the bus joined the A1 northbound it built up to its cruising speed. A large workforce were busily clearing up the coal spillage on the southbound carriageway. She amused herself by thinking that these burly men would rather be clearing up spillages in a wine shop, especially in this heat. She also noticed that, in the time it had taken her to visit Ashington, the tailback had grown to at least fifty cars. Some drivers had decided to wait for the road to reopen and were sitting on the grass verge enjoying the sun. She suspected that, had it been raining, these drivers would have taken the detour recommended by the police.

As the bus approached Holy Island there was no sign of the tide coming in yet. Finally, the bus dropped her off at Lindisfarne. As Marjorie was a spinster with no family to rush home and tend to, she decided to go straight to the Rectory. Rufus walked down the path to greet her, clearly tired from her earlier exertions at the beach. Once she realised there was nothing of interest in Marjorie's shopping basket, Rufus bounced back to her owners, who were taking afternoon tea underneath a garden umbrella in the rectory garden. All the summer flowers were out in full bloom and bees and numerous varieties of butterflies were busily moving between an array of asters, dahlias, roses and lavender. A wasp's nest had also appeared at the back of the apple trees, but fortunately Rufus showed little interest in this. As Marjorie opened the gate Mrs Collins called out to her.

'Perfect timing! Would you like to join us for afternoon tea on this quintessentially British summer's day?'

'Yes, please! That would be lovely.'

Once they were all seated and supplied with a welcoming cup of tea, Marjorie retold her day. As she prepared to talk about the wine shop, she said,

'It is best you are both sitting down for this. You see, when I was standing in the shop I had a little mishap.'

They both enquired as to whether she was ok.

'Yes, I'm fine, thank you. I have two items in my basket. I would like you to remain seated and open them at the same time.'

She passed each of the wrapped bottles of wine to the reverend and his wife for them to open simultaneously. Rufus was watching her master attentively. Once they were both unwrapped, the reverend and Mrs Collins read the labels. Reverend Collins was the first to speak.

'Good Lord! "Serafim-Santos, Fine Wines, Algarve, Portugal."'

Mrs Collins was also astounded. Marjorie then revealed how she had dropped a bottle in the shop and how kind the owners were. The reverend joked that he was glad he was forewarned to be careful, as he may well have dropped the bottle too.

'How fortunate that your bus was diverted, Marjorie!'

Marjorie then took out of her purse the business card she was given and passed it to the reverend.

'This might be helpful in trying to contact the family?'

'Thank you so much, Marjorie, this is wonderful news! We shall use these bottles for communion at this week's service! I will ring the Archbishop in the morning and ask if his contacts in London can continue the search.'

The three of them spent the rest of the afternoon in a jovial mood, wondering where things would lead next.

Part One

Dunstan Steads, Early 14th Century

Chapter 10

A Young Agnes

It was an early spring morning and a lone wolf tilted back its head and howled into the rising sun. There was a gentle breeze and the waves gently rolled onto the beach just north of Craster village. A young couple made love in an alcove behind the Scotch pine woodland and it was here that Agnes Weaver was conceived. Her father never got to hold his daughter in his arms, falling victim to the Black Death before she was born nine months later. Her mother brought her up the best she could by seeking residence in one of the houses in the fishing community.

In 1312, it was announced that the earl, Thomas of Lancaster, was to start construction of a castle on the coast between the villages of Embleton and Craster the following year. After the disaster at Bannockburn in 1314, a significant victory for the Scottish in their battle for independence, King II Edward submitted to Lancaster, who in effect became ruler of England. He attempted to govern for the next four years, but was unable to keep order or prevent the Scottish from raiding and retaking territory in the North.

By 1315 Agnes was an orphan, as her mother had passed away from typhus. At the age of fifteen she became one of the first kitchen maids to work at the partially completed Dunstanburgh Castle. She received next to no pay and worked fifteen hours a day, seven days a week to help feed the construction workers and the castle's ever-growing number of occupants. As she held no seniority in the kitchen she was treated cruelly by the castle cook, who often beat her if she made even the slightest mistake. She missed her mother and wished for a better life. The long shifts working in a hot kitchen left her exhausted, but the wonderful smells in there included roast pheasant, hare and salmon, which were often cooked in wild herbs including garlic. Roast swan was cooked on special occasions. Her passion for cooking was the only thing that kept her going.

By the time she was eighteen she had become a beautiful young woman with startling green eyes. However, she disguised her beauty to discourage the advances of the castle's ever-growing male population. Each day seemed to blend in to the next. Each time a storm's huge violent waves crashed against the cliffs below the castle she contemplated ending her short life by throwing herself off the cliff into the waters below.

Little did she know that her life was suddenly about to change...

Chapter 11

A Young Hugh

HUGH Parrock was born in Newcastle in 1298 to a middle-class military family that had both influence and money. At the age of fifteen, he followed his father's footsteps into the army. Although his father was a great soldier but, unlike his two elder brothers, Hugh had little interest in the military.

In 1318, aged twenty, Hugh's company was ordered north to reinforce the soldiers at the garrison near Berwick-upon-Tweed. This had been taken by the Scottish army in April, during the First War of Scottish Independence. Their horses were loaded with supplies and messages to be delivered to the Earl of Lancaster en route at Dunstanburgh Castle. The site had excellent sea defences and took advantage of existing earthworks from a previous Iron Age fort.

They spent their first night at Warkworth Castle, which was originally made of a feeble wooden construction in the early thirteenth century and would have its garrisons reinforced in a few years' time. Hugh and his fellow soldiers spent an enjoyable evening consuming great quantities of wine and eating a roasted pig, all provided by their host. The next day, Hugh and his companions mounted their horses and headed north on the coastal tracks towards Dunstanburgh Castle. On that particular morning, the castle cook was in a particularly bad mood and took his anger out on Agnes.

'You lazy urchin! Why have you not yet prepared the food for lunch? We have important military visitors today!'

'I have been working, sir, since first daylight.'

With this he beat Agnes, but she dared not cry as this would rile him more. The other kitchen staff started to work faster, eager to avoid the wrath of the head chef. By two o'clock, Hugh had arrived at Dunstanburgh Castle with his fellow troops. A banquet lunch was served in the courtyard by the kitchen staff. Hugh noticed a sad, timid, young woman with bruises on her arm bringing out some of the tin plates. Their eyes met and he smiled back at her. She quickly looked away, not wanting to attract the attention of the cook.

The banquet was a riotous one, and copious amounts of wine were consumed. A jester entertained Hugh and his fellow soldiers. Music was played, poems read out and the party continued into the early hours of the morning. Around 5am the next morning while Hugh's group were sleeping off their hngovers, Agnes awoke after only five hours' sleep to prepare the breakfasts for the castle occupants and guests. She expected to find the cook in the kitchen, but he was nowhere to be seen. The early summer sunlight was already shining through the windows. She picked up a knife and walked over to her bench to start preparing the food, but froze in terror as she saw the cook on the floor next to her kitchen bench. She knelt down on the cold flagstone and gently checked to see if he was breathing. Although she hated this vile, cruel creature she wished him no harm. Much to her alarm, she was unable to find any sign of life. At this moment, several of the kitchen staff entered the room. They all saw Agnes kneeling next to the cook with a knife in her hand.

'Agnes! What have you done?' One of the kitchen workers called out.

'Nothing! I found him like this.'

One of the other junior servants screamed and ran out into the courtyard, knocking over a wicker basket of freshly-caught fish.

'Murder! Murder!'

Hugh woke from his dreamy drunken stupor, wondering what all the commotion was.

'Did I just hear someone shout murder, or was I dreaming?'

'Murder! Murder!' he heard again.

By now, most of the guards were awake. Hugh brushed away the last remnants of sleep, quickly got up from his straw mattress, and spoke to the hysterical woman.

'Calm yourself, miss. What seems to be the problem?'

'Sir, Agnes has killed the cook. He's dead!'

By now adrenalin had kicked in and Hugh's hangover seemed to have temporarily abated.

'Take me there at once!'

The woman led Hugh towards the kitchen. By now the castle constable was also awake and he too was en route to the kitchen, where they both arrived at the same time.

Agnes stood quiet in the corner, away from the kitchen staff gathered around the dead cook. When the soldiers came in they all pointed at Agnes and said, in unison,

'She killed Cook! She had a knife in her hand and was standing over his body!'

The castle constable, Robert of Binchester, was a fearsome-looking individual. Agnes now faced his wrath.

'Is this true, woman?'

'No, sir! I arrived for work and found him like this!'

'Liar!' shouted another servant.

'She hates him! Everyone knows that.'

None of the other kitchen staff particularly liked Agnes and were jealous of the unwanted attention she seemed to have from male members of the castle, despite her attempts to make herself inconspicuous.

Constable Binchester was a cruel and vindictive person, despised by the castle guards and workers alike. As a child, his father had instilled in him never to show any weakness, as people would use this against him, and that cruelty would command respect. He had an air of authority and arrogance about him; he stood tall, stroking his beard as he contemplated what to do next.

Hugh decided to intervene. He approached Agnes and spoke to her calmly.

'Miss, tell me what happened, please.'

'Sir, I found him like this, honest. I never touched him.'

By now, Constable Binchester had made a decision. He would not ignore the comments of the other staff and an unresolved murder on his watch would not look favourably upon him. He thought it was unlikely she had killed the cook and, as he had previously decided to use the pretty young woman for his lustful desires whether she liked it or not, thought it would be a shame to have her incarcerated. What no one had pointed out was that there was no blood on the knife and the chef had no stab wounds, or any visible wounds at all. The constable was keen to arrest someone and Agnes was the obvious choice.

'Agnes Weaver,' he announced. 'I hereby arrest you on the charge of murder. You will be detained at the gaol in Hexham until your trial!'

Confused and scared, Agnes did not protest as she was unceremoniously dragged away to face her fate.

Hugh tried to intervene but was strongly advised by one of the castle guards not to interfere in matters that did not concern him. He, too, was observant enough to notice that there was no blood on the knife and the no visible stab wounds. Hugh thought the cook looked decrepit, and thought that he had probably died of natural causes.

Constable Binchester had not paid a great deal of attention to Hugh.

Chapter 12

The Arrest

AGNES was handcuffed and dispatched from the castle in the back of a horse carriage. She had heard horror stories from the newly constructed Hexham Gaol. Apparently, the judge enjoyed issuing cruel punishments, especially to those convicted of witchcraft. The best Agnes could hope for would be a swift, painless end to her short life.

The journey to Hexham took two days, during which she was given no food and only a small ration of water. By the time she arrived at the gaol, she was exhausted. The two guards handed Agnes over to the gaoler and a trial was set for one week's time.

Agnes was chained to a wall in a damp cell lit only by a small window near the ceiling. Her only company for the next week would be a woman charged with witchcraft and several rats who would scurry around the floor looking for any scraps of food.

The food served through a hatch was a cold concoction of watered-down meat and vegetables that even the rats would find difficult to consume. Two tin bowls were left once a day along with a mug of filthy water. The chains were tight on her wrists and her pleas to the gaoler were pointless. He was clearly sadistic; he greatly enjoyed listening to the pleas of the inmates and revelled in telling them what their punishments were likely to be. The so-called witch who shared her cell clearly had no magical powers and was, sadly, just an insane woman who had been charged with witchcraft. Punishments for such people were particularly cruel.

Agnes thought that at least she would meet her fate quickly and within a week she would be joining her mother. Each night she prayed in her cell.

Chapter 13

A Concerned Hugh

Hugh's company was due to head north to Berwick after a few days' rest. Although he had been previously warned not to interfere with castle matters, he could not stop thinking about the young woman called Agnes with the sparkling green eyes. If only he could find a way to help her! He thought that if, perhaps, he could get word to the Earl of Lancaster himself, he could convince him of her innocence. But he knew this was a ridiculous idea as, first, Hugh was of a low rank and second, the earl was away fighting against King Edward II and he would not be back to see his nearly completed castle any time soon.

Hugh spotted Constable Binchester and decided to speak to him.

'Sir, this is none of my business, but may I enquire as to the fate of the kitchen woman? I noticed there was no blood on the supposed murder weapon.'

'Do not trouble yourself with matters that do not concern you! She is currently being held at the new gaol at Hexham and is to be tried for murder next week.'

'I've heard that the judge at Hexham has never found anyone not guilty', the constable continued, with a smile on his face. 'So I'd best ask the new cook to get another kitchen servant! I suggest you continue your journey north to Berwick where you can be of use.'

Constable Binchester then recalled that Hugh had been in the kitchen the day he had Agnes arrested. He called back to Hugh, who was walking away.

'Soldier! What is your name?'

'Hugh Parrock, sir.'

'Don't forget, Parrock, castle matters here are not your concern.'

'Aye, sir.'

Constable Binchester took an instant dislike to this impertinent young soldier and would report this to his commanding officer. He would also remember his face.

Hugh was uncertain of what to do, as Agnes's fate seemed certain, although he was convinced of her innocence. He walked down to the beach between Craster and Embleton, trying to think of a plan that would save her. One of his fellow men, whom he had known since childhood, joined him on the beach. Unlike Hugh, Thomas was enthusiastic about the army and was keen to advance through the ranks.

'What's troubling you, Hugh?'

'The girl, Thomas, the one charged with the murder in the castle kitchen. Do you think she is innocent?'

'Possibly, but that's not our concern. We need to start heading north soon with the rest of the men.'

'Thomas, you are my oldest friend and I trust you. Will you help me?'

'Of course, you only have to ask.'

'I will not be accompanying you to Berwick. I want you to cover for me. It's best you don't know what I have planned. Just cover for me, that's all.'

'Aye, Hugh, as you wish. You make a rubbish soldier anyway – you're always trying to save people!'

This was indeed true. Hugh had always shown empathy towards others.

Thomas and the others left the next day. There were over two hundred people in the group, so it would be some time before Hugh's disappearance would be noticed and he trusted Thomas to cover for him.

He quickly mounted his horse and headed towards Hexham, where he wanted to witness Agnes's trial. He was hoping that the judge would take pity; at this stage Hugh was unsure of his own plans. He tried to avoid all human contact during his journey. Once he had arrived in the town he took up lodgings at the local inn. Hugh made discrete enquiries and heard that Agnes's trial had been set for three days' time. There was nothing to do but to wait at the inn. He declined all the wine as he needed a clear head. Although he wasn't hungry, he dined on roast pheasant with cabbage onions and crusty bread in order to keep his strength up.

No one asked any questions, but the looks on some people's faces indicated they knew he could be a deserter from the army. He made a mental note to purchase some more ordinary clothes in the morning, so he could blend more easily into the crowds.

Chapter 14

The Gaol

AGNE'S wrists were sore from the chains attached to the wall. The cell was particularly cold at night and her companion's murmurings kept her awake for hours. The metal cell door opened and the gaoler entered, spat in her food and then placed its contents beside her.

'Enjoy your last supper!' he crowed. 'I hope the judge finds a fitting punishment for you tomorrow!'

As he left the cell, he kicked Agnes in the ribs and threw food all over the 'witch', causing her to wail frantically for the next hour. That final night seemed to last an eternity. At eight o'clock the next morning, four gaol guards entered the cell. Two grabbed Agnes and the other two took the 'witch'. They were marched to the town square where they were chained to posts on a raised platform opposite the stand where the judge and his advisors would sit. Already a large crowd had gathered, most of whom were taunting the two defendants.

'Off with their heads!'

'Burn the witch!'

Hugh took a place at the back of the crowd and remained silent. At just before nine o'clock, the judge climbed onto the stage along with his four advisors. The town prosecutor then arrived. Agnes and the 'witch' would have to defend themselves.

The town crier took to the stage.

'Hear ye! Hear ye! Silence for the Court!'

The judge and his four advisors sat down. The crowd stood silently, not wanting to miss any of the proceedings. The judge then looked at the prosecutor and asked,

'What is the first case today?'

The prosecutor pointed to the 'witch'.

'M'Lord, this woman you see before you is charged with witchcraft. She is accused of casting spells on the townsfolk of Hexham and promoting Satan.'

The judge looked towards the 'witch' and asked,

'What is your name and how do you plead to the charges?'

She stared at the judge in silence for over two minutes. She then titled back her head and started to scream gibberish.

The judge called for silence. The woman screamed even louder.

'Silence I say!'

One of the guards hit her with a stick and the crowd recoiled as they heard the bone in her arm break. She stopped crying and began to whimper quietly.

The crowds, keen to see a macabre punishment, were growing impatient.

'Off with her head!'

'Burn her!'

'Hang her!'

This time the town crier called for silence.

The judge was clearly becoming impatient and, once silence had been restored, made his decision without consulting his advisors.

'Woman with no name, I find you guilty of witchcraft and hereby sentence you to death by boiling water at noon today!'

The crowd was clearly pleased with the verdict and cheered the judge. Even his advisors, who had not been consulted, nodded their approval. The woman had started to scream again but was taken back to the gaol to prepare for her punishment.

Once the crowd was quiet, the judge asked the prosecutor, 'And what is the second case here today?'

'Your Honour, the woman you see before you is charged with murdering her employer, a cook at Dunstanburgh Castle. Constable Binchester arranged for her transportation here and she has been detained at the gaol while awaiting her trial here today.'

A petrified Agnes remained silent while the charge was read out. She held her head high and looked around the crowd, hoping that they would take pity on her. Despite her innocence, Agnes was aware that her life was about to end, knowing that all people charged were always found guilty.

The judge looked at Agnes once the charges had been read out and asked,

'What is your name and how do you plead to the charge of murder?'

Again, the crowd was silent as they waited for her response. It was unusual for people to plead guilty regardless of their innocence or not, so the crowd were anticipating the standard reply.

Chapter 15

The Verdict

Hugh wanted to shout that she was innocent but knew it would be futile and, in any case, he would possibly be arrested for desertion. In a clear and angelic voice she replied,

'Your Honour, my name is Agnes Weaver and I plead not guilty to the charge.'

The judge consulted his advisors and made his decision promptly.

'Agnes Weaver this court finds you guilty of murder and I hereby sentenced you to drowning at Embleton in ten days' time. May God forgive you for your sins. Court is adjourned.'

The crowd dispersed quickly – after all, the bloodthirsty people had the boiling of a witch to witness at noon that day. It was unlikely that anyone would make the day-long journey to see Agnes's death, as the drowning of a young woman did not provide as much sadistic entertainment. One person, however, would be there and he intended to save her, however he could.

The judge walked across the stage and spoke quietly to Agnes as he left.

'Whether you are innocent or not, young woman, I must preserve my reputation as a strict upholder of the law. Please forgive me if you are innocent; I have chosen the least painful punishment for you. Good day.'

Still in shock, Agnes didn't know whether to thank him for sentencing her to death or scream that she was innocent. She knew any action would be futile, so she held her head high and waited for the guards to return her to the gaol.

Hugh now knew what he had to do. He left the crowd quickly, not wanting to be seen. He mounted his horse at the inn and set off on the two-day gallop north to meet his company and friend Thomas.

Agnes, meanwhile, had resigned herself to her forthcoming fate by the time she had been returned to her cell. Her cell companion, the witch, would soon be free from this life and then at peace. She said a prayer for her, knowing that she, like herself, was innocent. Even the gaol guard seemed to have changed; this time the chains were not as tight around her wrists and he did not try and goad her like he had previously.

The clock struck noon, and Agnes heard the agonising screams of her cellmate as she was boiled alive. She could also hear the barbaric crowd cheer. Mercifully, the screams did not last long. She could not imagine what this poor woman had gone through. She covered her ears in an attempt to block out the sound of the crowd.

Agnes was not hungry, but she forced a small amount of gruel down and lay down on the straw that covered the floor. She fell into a deep sleep where waves of gentle water were rolling over her head. She slept soundly that night, something she had not experienced in a long time, and dreamed of the rare kind man at the castle who believed she was innocent. She did not even know his name. Little did she know that Hugh had been at the back of the crowd earlier that day witnessing her fate.

After the farcical trial, Hugh had left the crowd and started his journey back to the coast. He changed back into his military attire from the less conspicuous outfit he had purchased that day, and stowed it in his travel satchel on his horse.

Chapter 16

A Goodbye

HUGH managed to stay undetected as he entered the garrison at Dunstanburgh Castle and quickly found his friend Thomas, who was finishing a meal of roast pheasant.

'Hugh! There you are. What took you so long?'

'Thomas, my dear friend, I intend to rescue that poor woman who has wrongly been sentenced to death next week.'

'Look, Hugh, you are a decent fellow but we can't always do the right thing. Just forget her.'

'Sadly, I can't. I have little time to save her. We are due to leave here tomorrow and I will disappear again at dawn. I just wanted to say goodbye, my dear and loyal friend, Thomas.'

'From the way you are talking I fear that we will not be meeting again.'

'Perhaps one day we will meet again. When you reach Berwick try not to get yourself killed by the Scots. I know my two brothers and father would relish a good battle but a military career is not for me. I know it will bring shame on my family but they will soon forget me and my mother is no longer here to witness these dark times.'

They both shook hands. Thomas pressed the last of his meagre military wages into Hugh's palm.

'Here, take this. It is not much but it should help. It is best I don't know your plans. If I am questioned I will think of a story to cover for you.'

'Thomas, I don't expect you to lie for me, but all delaying tactics would be appreciated.'

At dawn the next morning, Hugh left Dunstanburgh Castle and rode his horse to Newcastle, where he would implement the next part of his plan. He hoped that Agnes was bearing up. He wasn't really sure what he would say to her if his plan were to succeed. He hoped that she would want to travel with him but would leave that choice to her. Fortunately, he had managed to sneak in and out of the castle without being noticed by Constable Binchester.

Chapter 17

Incarceration

THE gaol guard's short-lived compassion had come to an end early that morning. Agnes now had a new cellmate that he could torment.

'I 'eard they boiled that old witch up proper good, took 'er sometime to stop screaming. You'll be next! The judge of Hexham will hold his court soon. Missy over there will be drowned by then!'

The guard left, having dropped their cold offering of food onto the cell floor. It was particularly hot this day and Agnes drank some of the foul-tasting water from the tankard. She had lost some weight since her incarceration, which had started to show on her slim build.

After a short period of time, Agnes's new cellmate spoke gently.

'Is...is it true you are to drown?'

'Yes, in a few days' time at Embleton. I've been wrongly convicted of murder. My name is Agnes.'

'Pleased to meet you, Agnes. I am Rose. You seem very calm considering the circumstances.'

'Resigned is a better word. And you, Rose? Why are you here?'

'I stole some bread from my master's kitchen to feed my family and was caught. My poor babies will starve!'

Rose started to cry. Agnes doubted that the cruel judge would show her mercy but kept her thoughts to herself. She tried to console her and told her everything should be alright. However, reality started to set in and she realised that she herself would be dead by the time Rose's trial had even started. Perhaps they would meet again in heaven soon. They passed the day idly talking about their respective lives, trying to forget what the next few days were likely to bring. They were discussing the men in their lives. Rose had been married to a carpenter for three years and they had two children. Agnes said she had no one in her life.

That night she suddenly remembered the name of the young man who had been so kind to her in the kitchen at Dunstanburgh Castle. Hugh! That was it. So far in her short life all men had been cruel to her. Her mother said her father was a gentle man. She recalled seeing a man that looked similar to Hugh at the back of the crowd during her trial. She couldn't be sure, but she hoped it was him.

If only he were here to comfort her now.

Chapter 18

Avoiding Family

HUGH arrived in Newcastle knowing that he had little time. He was especially wary of meeting any of his family and avoided all human contact where possible. Although he was from a wealthy middle-class family, he himself was not particularly affluent. His two elder brothers were following closely in their father's footsteps and, as his beloved mother had succumbed to the plague, he would not miss his family and was sure they felt the same. He knew his father and brothers would be at the city barracks during the day, so he sneaked into the family home via the backstreet entrance and avoided the house servants.

Once inside his old room, he retrieved his life savings from behind a wooden panel. The leather bag contained five gold coins which, he thought, should have been enough for what he had planned. He could hear the house servants downstairs, chatting and laughing. He looked around his old room for what he thought would be the last time. The morning sun shone through the windows of the half-timber house, casting a warm glow on all the objects in the room.

As he left the room, the floor boards under his feet started to creak. He froze, not wanting to alert the servants below. Fortunately, they were having a raucous time while their master was away. Hugh once again joined the street at the rear of the house and set off towards the harbour.

While he was walking and trying to avoid people he may have known, he thought of Agnes.

She would be en route to the coast by now in preparation for her drowning in a few days' time. He hoped that she had not come to any harm on her journey, as the castle sentries were often cruel and gave little value to human life.

Chapter 19

Transporting the Prisoner

THE gaoler entered the cell accompanied by two guards.

'It is time!' he shouted.

Rose started to cry and thanked Agnes for all the kindness she had shown her.

'Good luck, Rose. I am sure the judge will show mercy on you.'

They both knew, however, that this would not be the case, as the judge had his reputation to uphold.

The two guards dragged Agnes roughly to the caged carriage outside. Having spent those last, miserable days in a damp and darkened cell, the bright sunshine was a real shock to her eyes. She began to squint and breathed in the fresh air. Agnes felt hungry but knew she had already eaten her last meal. She lay down on the hard, strawless carriage floor as it made its journey towards the coast. As the carriage left Hexham, some of the locals shouted obscenities at her. Most of them called her a witch and were disappointed that they would not get to witness a gruesome death. Once outside the town, the carriage joined the dusty track to the northeast for the overnight stop.

There was no protection from the summer heat as it shone into the carriage. Although Agnes had told Rose she was not frightened of dying, she now admitted to herself that she was. She feared the water, as did the majority of people living by the sea. She was not sure what to expect from drowning. Would it be painful?

Witches that were tried and found guilty were sometimes sentenced to drownings. This punishment, however, was usually reserved for murderers. They were told that if they survived drowning they must be a witch and would then be burned alive. This fact was never questioned.

The carriage stopped for a midday rest. The two guards did not acknowledge Agnes or offer her any water. Her mouth was dry and she watched them with envy as they drank cool water from a freshwater spring. It looked so inviting compared with what she had been served at the gaol.

She could not hear what they were talking about, but when they laughed they pointed at her. She suspected it was not good news and a chill went down her spine even on this gloriously hot day. The air was hot and sticky and it felt like a thunderstorm was imminent.

After an hour, the guards resumed their journey. They were eerily quiet after their earlier antics. En route to the evening stop, they passed several other horses and carts travelling south to sell their wares at Hexham market.

The hedgerows were full of lush leaves and wild flowers that grew beside the edge of the track. In fact, all the vegetation was in desperate need of a good rainfall. Two juvenile male hares were boxing in patch of grass near a stream that followed the track. A pheasant that had been hiding was disturbed by a fox looking for an easy meal and flew up into the air.

After six more hours of travelling in the stifling heat, the carriage approached its stopping point for that night.

Chapter 20

A Negotiation

As Hugh arrived at the Port of Newcastle, he looked for the trade cogs which frequently travelled to London. There he would be able to implement the next part of his plan. Hugh walked slowly past the fishnets drying along the seafront towards the trade cogs. These vessels were used for transporting the coal that was mined in County Durham and the open cast mines at Shotton in Northumberland. He listened as their captains shouted orders to the crew. Hugh walked up and down the harbour front twice before selecting the cog captain he thought would be the most amenable to his request.

'Permission to come aboard, Captain?'

'Aye, come aboard, lad.'

'Captain, I have a business opportunity for you which could benefit us both.'

'Aye, go on, lad. I'm listening.'

'When are you due to sail to London next?'

'My ship is currently half full and once the horses have arrived from Shotton and loading is complete I will be ready to set sail. We'll leave on the high tides in three days' time when the church at Wallsend strikes midnight. Since the cathedral was destroyed by fire, we have to rely on other churches for the time. Why do you ask?'

'I wish you to carry two items of extra cargo which must not appear on your manifest.'

'Look, sonny, I don't want any trouble. The last person who smuggled wool flax from this port was hung. Sorry, I'm not interested.'

'Captain, I should have said, the cargo is myself and one other person. The journey will be one way. I will pay you one gold coin now for the both of us and one coin on arrival.'

Hugh thought he could detect a small smile on the captain's face. Two gold coins was a large payment and he knew it.

'Well, it sounds too good to be true. I set sail when the Wallsend bells strike twelve, with or without you.'

'Thank you, Captain, I appreciate your help and discretion.'

Hugh discreetly passed one gold coin to the captain. He knew he had paid him handsomely and the knowledge that he would receive another one in London was an incentive enough for the captain to see his side of the bargain through. Smuggling two people was much easier than wool flax.

'Don't forget, sonny, I sail at midnight at high tide in three days with or without you. And your fare is non-refundable.'

'I understand, Captain. I will be here. See you then.'

Hugh walked back to the stable where he had left his horse. He paid the stable boy one groat for looking after his horse and asked to speak to the stable owner. He then went to find his master. The stables were home to just over a dozen horses. Hugh thought to himself that his horse was by far the finest specimen among them. Two horses were housed in each stable and they were clearly well looked after. The stable owner arrived shortly afterwards, followed by the stable boy.

'Yes, sir, how may I help?'

'I have a proposition for you.'

The owner quickly dismissed the stable boy, not wanting him to hear what was about to be offered.

'Boy, go and clean out the end stable!'

'Aye, sir!'

'I will be returning in a few days' time and I will be selling this fine mare, if you are interested?'

'Aye, I might be if the price is right. How much do you want?'

Hugh knew the horse was worth at least one hundred silver coins and didn't want to raise suspicion by asking too little.

'One hundred and ten silver coins.'

The stable owner paused briefly and then burst out laughing.

'The way I see it, the fine specimen is suspiciously like a military horse. And no one would really want to sell her if she wasn't. However, if you are keen to sell...I may be interested for, shall we say, forty silver coins?'

Hugh pondered this offer. After paying the cog captain two gold coins this would leave him three gold, forty silver, and some loose groats which equated to almost six gold coins. He hoped this would be enough for the next part of his journey.

'Fifty and no more questions?'

The stable owner smiled, knowing he was about to get an exceptional bargain

'Forty-five and no more questions.'

Hugh knew that he had little choice but to accept the low price. But considering it wasn't his to sell, he just hoped the mare who had served him well would go to a good home. Feeling slightly guilty, he reluctantly replied,

'Aye, forty-five silver coins. I shall return in three days' time.'

'Aye, see you then. Boy! Have you finished cleaning that stable yet?'

Hugh left the stables and rode his horse on the coastal road. He camped just south of Craster that night.

Chapter 21

The Opportunists

THE caged carriage transporting Agnes to the coast stopped that night at Nunnykirk along the banks of the River Font. As she was deemed a low-profile prisoner, there was only a horseman and one guard. They lit a campfire beside the river and ate a supper of wild rabbit. They finally offered Agnes some water from a jug, which she drank despite its warmth, but they did not speak to her and she dared not say anything to them. Later, the two guards approached the carriage and began to talk to Agnes.

'How are ye going to pay for the water we gave you, eh?'

Agnes sensed a change in their mood. She started to move to the other corner of the carriage, not daring to speak.

'You hear me? Are you deaf, you murdering scum?'

The other guard was already wine-drunk and decided to join in.

'Perhaps you could offer something as payment!'

The other guard made a lewd suggestion with a tree branch.

'Perhaps you would like the real thing!'

'I bet she's as fresh as the morning dew!'

Agnes had always tried to hide her good looks as she did not want any advances from the cruel, male castle residents. She had heard the castle maid talking about the antics they got up to with the castle sentries. She had wondered what it would be like to be touched by a man, but she did not intend to allow these vile guards to come near her. She would put up a brave fight if necessary, but her skin began to crawl and she felt terrified.

"Ere, she looks scared!'

They both started to laugh and tormented her further.

'Not sure if we should touch her. Criggle has promised me six coins if we deliver her unharmed.'

'That old toad! I thought he had died of syphilis?'

'Nah, he's still going. Just think, with six coins we could have a night of debauchery at the castle.'

'Why not have both?'

'Nah, not worth the risk. Criggle would know and then we would get no money.'

'Shame, but you are right.'

'You better get some rest, missy. You will need your energy when Criggle has his wicked way with you. He's a real looker!'

The guards soon became bored of tormenting her and sat by the fire drinking wine. Agnes was shivering in the carriage during the night, partly due to fear and in part from the cold. She had the indignity of having to urinate in the carriage. She tried to pick the lock of her chains but it was a pointless exercise. Sores had started to appear on her ankles. She wished the kind man, Hugh, were there and prayed that she would not ever have to meet the man they called Criggle. The guards slept soundly and nosily, sleeping off their large wine intake. Throughout the night, she listened to the barn owls, calling to one another nearby, and the distinct sound of howling wolves. A fox also walked up to the camp fire looking for any morsels of food, but moved away from the area after finding none.

Agnes stayed awake all night in case they changed their minds.

Chapter 22

A Plan Unfolds

HUGH woke early that morning and rode into Embleton as the shopkeepers were opening up for the day. He tied his horse in a copse just outside of the village, trying to keep a low profile.

The first store he entered sold an array of food produce. He knew that if he could rescue Agnes she would be hungry, so he purchased two cheeses and dried rabbit meat along with four bread rolls.

He enquired as to whether the shopkeeper sold wine. He didn't, so Hugh was advised to try the store in the main street. Hugh thanked the shopkeeper and paid for the goods, entering the next shop shortly afterwards. The hares, rabbits and pheasants hanging up outside were fresh, having been killed early that morning. Local hunters sold their surplus food to either local shops or markets.

'Good morning. Have you any really strong wine for sale?'

'Aye, lad. Depends if you are particular with the taste or just want to get blinding drunk!'

'Blinding drunk would be perfect; I will have two pitchers please.'

'Well, laddie, you'll be having a rotten time of it the next day!'

The shopkeeper put the heavy wine pitchers on the counter. They were filled to the brim with cheap but extremely potent alcohol.

Having paid, Hugh walked down line of trees overlooking Dunstanburgh Castle. He could see chains attached to the rock. After he had hidden the jugs and checked he wasn't being followed, he walked down to the beach. The rocks formed a curved hump as they dropped into the sea. This bizarre formation looked out of place. The strip of rock was actually formed from volcanic activity many years ago, and it was known locally as Greymare Rock. The chains were attached on the northern face of the rock, obscured from the castle windows. This was a stroke of luck and would be of great benefit to Hugh's plan.

Once he was familiar with the area, Hugh returned to the tree-line undetected. He then returned to Embleton to collect his horse and the saddlebag which contained his food purchases.

To avoid any further unnecessary suspicion from the locals, Hugh rode his horse south, then west, and northeast to the woods where he had hidden the wine. He then fed his horse and ensured his mare had drunk plenty from the freshwater stream which ran into the sea. He wanted the horse to rest for as long as possible as she would need all her strength the next day.

Having tended to his horse, he went over to the pitchers of wine. Although they were almost visibly identical, Hugh made a discreet scratch on the side of one with a pebble so he would not get them mixed up. He then emptied the contents of the scratched pitcher into the ground. There was a pungent smell of alcohol and he did not doubt its strength. He then washed out the empty pitcher in the stream before placing the empty vessel next to the full one full of wine.

Hugh could not risk lighting a fire that night, as it would attract the attention of the castle sentries. All he could do was wait for the following day to arrive. Hugh fell into a deep sleep after darkness and did not intend to rise early, as he knew the next day would be extremely busy and he had a boat to catch the following night. He hoped that Agnes would be with him.

Chapter 23

The Dungeons

The two guards woke early that same day to complete the final part of Agnes's journey from Nunnykirk to the castle. The guards were in high spirits, keen as they were to return to the coast and complete their deal with Criggle. The familiar smell of the salty air, which was slightly cooler than that inland, told Agnes that they were approaching the coast.

Early in the evening, the carriage arrived at the castle gates where Constable Binchester was already waiting.

'I hope you had an uncomfortable journey, you murderous scum! Are you looking forward to a little water tomorrow?'

Agnes ignored the jibes.

'Guards! Take her to the castle dungeons for her final night.'

In all the time Agnes had worked in the kitchens she had never visited the dungeons, but had heard stories of cruel torture devices and of long-term prisoners often succumbing to madness.

The two guards dragged Agnes roughly into a windowless cell at the bottom of the staircase and slammed the door closed. She huddled in the corner and tried to rest, but she could hear movement. It was either a cockroach or a rat. When something ran over her toes she screamed. It was a cockroach; if a rat or its fleas had bitten her, she may well have been infected with the bubonic plague but she would not have cared as she was about to die anyway.

After what seemed like several hours, Agnes drifted off into a light sleep. She was extremely hungry and her mouth was dry from a lack of water. Tomorrow her life was scheduled to end and this nightmare would be over. She was sure that no one could save her now.

Chapter 24

Prisoner for Sale

The morning of Agnes's scheduled death was particularly muggy. Her cell door opened at the crack of dawn to reveal a priest poised to read her last rites. He passed a jug of water to her, tears pooling in her eyes.

She gulped noisily from the jug. Before she could drink more than half, a guard stormed into the cell and knocked it from her hand. It shattered into hundreds of pieces and quickly soaked into the damp floor.

'No privileges for the prisoner!'

The priest said his goodbyes and left the cell.

The flickering candles outside in the corridor provided the only light.

The two guards who had transported her from Hexham then arrived. They were in a joyful mood, clearly pleased that Criggle could finally make good on their deal.

Hugh, meanwhile, awoke after a restful sleep, aware that today he would see Agnes again. He prayed that he could save her. He tended to his well-rested horse and then ate a breakfast of bread and cheese before drinking more water from the cold stream.

Shortly afterwards, the two guards dragged Agnes to Greymare Rock, accompanied by Constable Binchester. Criggle was already there, waiting.

Constable Binchester was the first to speak.

'There you are, Criggle! This is the woman to be drowned. Chain her up once the tide starts to go out. She must not drown until the tide returns again. Do you understand?'

'Aye, sir, I do. I will ensure she waits the day out in the heat!'

'Good! Then I shall return after dark to see her drown at high tide.'

This method of psychological torture was often used in drowning punishments. The prisoner would have to wait for the tide to go out completely and watch it come back in again. Most would scream and panic and beg for clemency when the returning tides drew close.

'Aye, sir, as you wish.'

Constable Binchester then turned his attention to Agnes.

'Agnes Weaver, you have been tried and found guilty of murder. As per order of the Court you are hereby sentenced to drowning today. You have been given your last rites. May God show you mercy!'

With that, he turned and went back to the castle in a remarkably good mood. He would return when the next high tide was due after dark, no doubt with a large group of witnesses.

Once the constable was out of hearing range, the two guards addressed the small, pockmarked man.

'You got our money, Criggle? She ain't been touched!'

Criggle grinned. To say he looked like a toad was not an exaggeration. The vile creature's face and head were covered in large boils and deformities from the advanced stages of syphilis.

'Yes, here are your coins!'

The guards snatched the money from Criggle, not wanting to touch him. They then pushed Agnes violently towards him. This took her by surprise and she fell over. She lay terrified on the floor, unable to move.

Hugh was watching these events from the tree-line. He could not hear the conversation but had seen Constable Binchester return to the castle. That left three people guarding her, which were too many for his plan to work. Any attack would create a commotion which would alert the castle sentries and it would all be over. He had to bide his time. Seeing Agnes pushed to the ground made him seethed with anger, but he knew he had to curb his emotions.

Shortly before midday, the tide had just passed its highest point and had started to recede. The two guards attached Agnes's chains to the ones on Greymare Rock. The water was surprisingly cold, even in the summer heat, and the water covered all their necklines. Agnes had to tilt her head back to stop the salty seawater from entering her mouth. The two guards climbed back to where Criggle was standing on dry land, both soaking wet.

'That's us done, Criggle! She's all yours. We're off to find ourselves some whores in the castle! Enjoy yourself; see you at high tide!'

The guards stripped off their tops so they could dry more easily in the sun.

Hugh observed their departure.

'Good' he thought. 'That just leaves one left'.

As the afternoon went on, the tide soon dropped below Agnes's ankles, and Criggle stood there ogling the wet clothing against her body, a leering grin stretched across his face.

The sentries at the castle gave a cursory glance at Greymare Rock each time they made their patrols. There had been little conflict at the castle, and their boredom had given way to complacency.

Criggle spoke to Agnes for the first time.

'Well, you are a pretty little thing, you. You're lucky you will get to experience Criggle's charms before you die. I am so looking forward to it!'

Agnes noticed his speech was slurred and suspected he was slightly intoxicated from the previous night.

Criggle stared at her but didn't say much else. This made Agnes uneasy, stood as she was, effectively at his mercy, chained to a rock and shivering in wet clothes.

Under the heat of the late afternoon sun, Hugh checked his mare was fed and watered. He stroked under her chin and the horse nuzzled him in return.

He decided now was the time to fill the empty wine pitcher with fresh cold water. He picked up the two pitchers – one full of wine, one without – and walked down to the beach obscured by the sand dunes. He took care not to be seen by the castle sentries or the Agnes's guard.

Hugh was now in earshot of Greymare Rock. He could see a sea otter running along the sandy beach with a large crab in its mouth. Seagulls were nosily squabbling over the scraps of dead fish left over by the receding tide. In fact, within an hour and a half the tide would be reaching its lowest point and then start to come back in.

Chapter 25

Criggle's Advances

Under the intensity of the early evening heat, Criggle found he could no longer contain his urges. Although high tide was still six hours away, he decided to make his move.

'It's about time you got to know me!'

Agnes was terrified and knew she would need all her strength and wits to fight him off. Her chains were a hindrance and she doubted that anyone would come to her rescue even if she could be heard screaming at the castle.

Hugh watched Criggle approach Agnes from his hiding place. He looked up at the castle and saw a sentry walking past a window. He could not let her suffer but would have to let the sentry pass. He had planned to talk to Agnes's guard several hours later, but would now have to take a chance in broad daylight.

By now, Criggle was standing in front of Agnes with a menacing grin on his potted face. He leaned in to kiss her and Agnes felt sick. He was utterly vile and his breath smelt of wine and stale onions. She turned her face away from him.

'Get away, you vile creature!'

'Don't ye find me handsome?'

Laughing, he tried to grab one of her breasts; Agnes pushed her head forward and bit hard into his nose. He screamed with agony, stepping backwards and holding his bloody nose. He could taste blood in his mouth and spat this out on to the beach.

'Bitch! You will be sorry you did that!'

Agnes could sense that she was about to be brutally attacked, and tried to think quickly. Criggle had regained his composure and started to walk towards her.

'Touch me again, you toad, and I will cast a spell on you!' she screamed. Criggle hesitated, but continued towards her once again. He was about to hit her when Agnes shouted,

'I willingly slept with both guards last night and, thanks to the spell I cast on them, their manhoods will fall off in two days' time!'

She tilted her head back and cackled in a manner she hoped would replicate the crazed laughter of a true witch.

Criggle was now cautious – he knew she had been tried for murder rather than witchcraft, but thought it was possible she could be one, all the same.

He retreated to a safe distance, further up the beach, where he contemplated his next move. The pain had receded slightly and he began to gently massage his nose. After a few minutes he spoke again.

'Perhaps when the water reaches your ankles you might change your mind and beg me to help. Drowning is too good a death for a witch like you. If you reverse the spell on my friends I might consider letting you go, but it will cost you.'

Agnes realised she had done enough for the time being to frighten him away, but she wasn't convinced this respite would last for long.

Chapter 26

The Drink

Hugh could hear and see what was happening but the sentry, whose attention was on the commotion below, was still visible, and would see him as soon as he left his hiding place. When Criggle reappeared the sentry moved away from the window. This was the moment Hugh made his move. He was impressed by Agnes's quick thinking, but thought she might not be able to dissuade him next time.

While Criggle was rubbing his nose and sulking, Hugh walked out from the sand dune he was hiding behind, carrying the two wine pitchers in one hand. His eyes darted between Agnes, Criggle and the castle window where the sentry would appear on his next patrol.

He caught Agnes's eye. She gasped when she recognised him. He quickly raised a finger of his free hand to his lips to warn her to be silent, but her gasp had already attracted Criggle's attention. Hugh was less than fifteen feet away when he was challenged by Criggle.

'What do you want?'

Hugh watched Criggle's right hand curl over a small dagger.

'Easy, there! I am a friend, not foe!'

'Answer my question, what d'ye want? Tell me before I stab ye with this!'

'My dear fellow, I am here to see this murderous scum drown for killing my brother!'

'The cook 'ad no brother!'

This gamble had not worked for Hugh – he had not expected this guard to have known the victim well.

'Well, actually, I am his cousin – but we were close as brothers.'

'He hated his family, thought his cousin was a tosser!'

Hugh laughed, trying to make his story sound convincing.

'That sounds like him, always had a sense of humour!'

At this Criggle laughed. Hugh was relieved that he was starting to believe him.

'You're not from around 'ere. Where ye from?'

Hugh tried to throw him off the scent, just in case this man was questioned later.

'Berwick. Can I offer you a drink? These are rather heavy!'

Criggle was still suspicious, but more relaxed, and the temptation of a free drink was too much for him to resist. Hugh sat down, making sure he was obscured from the castle sentry's view. Before Criggle sat down, Hugh passed him the pitcher of wine. Fortunately, Criggle remained in full view of the window, so no suspicion would arise.

Agnes thought to herself that a Hugh was an utter pig. He was related to her cruel employer and he was only here to drink and watch her die. She had been convinced that he was different, but, oh, how wrong she had been.

Hugh looked over at Agnes. Strange, he thought, she didn't look at all pleased to see him. In fact, did she just scowl at him? He had hoped she would return his feelings and would run away with him. Regardless of her choice he still intended to free her. He thought they had a mutual physical attraction and was confused by her nonchalant actions.

Criggle took his first swig from his pitcher, not bothering to eat his evening meal of bread and dried fish.

'This is good stuff.'

Hugh took a gulp of his water and agreed.

'So, you are here to see the bitch drown!'

'Aye! Let's drink to that!'

They both took a gulp from their respective pitchers.

Hugh was thinking of toasts he could make to his fictitious cousin, Criggle was enthusiastically drinking to them, and by seven o'clock both pitchers were empty. Hugh was concerned this man had hollow legs and thought perhaps he should have bought four pitchers.

Agnes was now resigned to her fate. She had watched the tide begin its slow, deadly approach. Only a short time, now, she thought to herself, and this agony will be over.

By now, Criggle's speech was slurred and his eyes looked bleary. He reeked of alcohol and sweat, and Hugh was relieved that the crisp sea air carried the smell away.

In the heat of the evening, Criggle finally succumbed to the potent strength of the cheap, strong wine. The sentry guard had recently completed a patrol, and there were still over four hours before high tide, when the crowds would appear and he would be relieved of his duties for the night.

Chapter 27

Reacquainted

CRIGGLE slumped forward and started to snore noisily. Hugh quickly grabbed a piece of driftwood from the hot dry, sand and leant over him. He used this y-shaped piece of wood to prop up Criggle's chin, so from the castle he would appear to be sitting upright. Once the other end of the wood was bedded into the sand, Hugh searched Criggle's body for the handcuff keys, taking them and his short dagger. He then leant close to Criggle's ear and whispered,

'I should kill you myself, you vile creature, for touching her! But I need you here, so will leave your destiny in the hands of your disease or your master!'

Hugh left a snoring Criggle propped up against the driftwood and walked towards Agnes. Hugh was holding the keys in one hand and the dagger in the other.

As he approached, Agnes she noticed that he did not stagger towards her, but walked with purpose.

'If you have come to avenge your cousin's death and kill me with that dagger, make it quick!'

'Good God, no, Agnes. I am here to rescue you. All that nonsense I spoke was a ploy to get the keys and free you!'

'I, I don't understand – you have been drinking and you are not drunk. I thought you were going to kill me?'

'No! The complete opposite. I was drinking cold water. We don't have much time. I will free you now and we can talk later.'

A sob rose in Agnes's throat as she realised that Hugh was different from other men and here to save her.

'Thank you! You are the kindest person I have ever met.'

Hugh knelt down, tucked the dagger into his trousers, and unlocked the chains that bound her ankles. The clasps had rusted slightly from the sea air but came loose with gentle persuasion. Agnes could feel the blood start to flow again. He then stood up and unlocked her hand chains, and once again she could feel the blood return to her wrists.

Chapter 28

Decision Required

HUGH dropped the keys and gently took her hand.
'Follow me, and keep low!'
Agnes gripped his hand and eagerly followed behind him. He didn't run, knowing she would be in discomfort after being chained up in one position for so long. Within five minutes they were in the sand dunes. Far out to sea there was a distant sound of thunder.

They soon arrived at the place where Hugh had hidden his horse in the wood. Hugh had been forced to act slightly ahead of schedule, which was not ideal, and he hoped the drunken guard would not wake before darkness. They would need as much time as possible to travel towards Newcastle, where the coal boat would be waiting.

Hugh stood and faced Agnes. He gently placed his hands on her shoulders before he spoke, and noticed her piercing green eyes for the first time.

'I know you are innocent, Agnes. That's why I have given you your freedom. I was at your trial and observed the proceedings. There was no evidence against you. The knife you were holding had no blood on the blade and I suspect the man died of natural causes. You have two choices. You can either take my horse with a little amount of money or travel with me far away from here.' In a hoarse voice, dry from the lack of water, Agnes responded,

'Thank you for believing in my innocence. I have to be honest, I am not sorry he had died as he was a cruel brute of a master. However, that's how I found him. And in answer to your question, please take me with you. I will miss the beautiful scenery but not its cruelty.'

She leant forward into Hugh's embrace.

'Oh, Agnes, I am so relieved you will be travelling with me!'

Fortunately, the rocks had shielded Agnes from some of the fierce sunshine of that day, but Hugh still noticed her sunburnt face.

'Forgive my manners! You must be hungry and so thirsty. Go to the stream to our right and drink the cool water. You can bathe there too. I, of course, will have my backed turned so you will have your privacy. I will prepare my horse and a meal for you before we depart. In my medical satchel I have a poultice of Marsh Marigold and goose fat, which you can apply to soothe your sunburns.'

'Well! Thank you, kind sir!'

Agnes smiled at Hugh and retreated to the stream as per his advice. She knelt down and pushed her head into the cool water, revelling in it for almost a minute. She drank copious amount of the cool liquid too.

While Agnes was at the stream, Hugh prepared them both a meal of bread and dried rabbit meat. He placed the sunburn poultice next to him as he sat with their food.

Agnes returned and sat down next to Hugh, their elbows touching.

'Please eat this. After you have finished, apply this to your skin, and I will prepare the horse for our departure.'

'I am not sure if I can come with you, Hugh.'

Hugh was shocked to hear this, but knew it was presumptuous of him to think that she would want to run away with him. Nervously, he replied,

'I am sorry if I have offended you in any way. I will gladly help you to escape to wherever you would like to go.'

A smile spread across Agnes's face.

'Oh no, I would love to, it's just...your food! I was a kitchen hand in the castle and I will need to give you lessons if I am to be persuaded to change my mind!'

Hugh was relieved to hear this and they both laughed together. After they had finished their food, Agnes applied the poultice while Hugh untied his horse, ready to leave.

Hugh jumped on his horse and held out his hand for Agnes. She noticed his strength as she took it and jumped up and sat behind him.

She put her arms around his waist as he commanded the horse to move. Hugh noticed the heat radiating from her hands as she clasped them around him.

Agnes placed great trust in Hugh, but as they moved away she asked,

'Just one question – where are we going?'

'Initially south, way south...'

Chapter 29

Criggle Sleeps

As evening fell, thunder and rain rolled over the coastal region. The beach where Criggle had been propped up became saturated with rainwater. The driftwood holding him up sank down into the sand and he collapsed in a heap.

At that moment, a bolt of lightning struck one of the castle's northern turrets, causing a small fire and panic within the castle walls. A sentry on his patrol looked out of his viewing window and noticed Criggle spread-eagled on the beach. He hoped he was just asleep, but decided to raise the alarm just in case it was something more sinister. He knew that Constable Binchester would be furious, as he had been clear in his instruction that he was not to be disturbed until the high tide was level with the castle.

The sentry blew three long blasts on the cow horn bugle to alert the castle of a security breach. Those who rushed to his location were told to wait there until he had spoken to Constable Binchester.

By now, the brief thunderstorm had passed inland and to the west. The small fire caused by the lightning strike had been extinguished using water contained in wooden buckets. The local stonemasons would be busy with the repairs over the next few weeks.

The sentry nervously knocked on ornate solid oak door that led to Constable Binchester's personal quarters.

'What is it? I specifically asked not to be disturbed until later.'

'Sir, I have raised the alarm as Criggle is not moving.' The sentry shouted back.

The door was wrenched open a few moments later. The constable was unclothed from the waist upwards and clearly had been in the throes of passion with a terrified looking scullery maid who was naked on a straw mattress. With his position of authority, he often forced the castle women to have afternoon liaisons with him. Those that had refused had scars to show for their resistance. He had recently taken an interest in Agnes, but her arrest had put a stop to his hopes of such an occasion.

'Hells bells and God's teeth man! You better pray this is a false alarm or heads will roll!'

He turned to the terrified maid on the mattress.

'Wait there, woman! I shall return!'

He grabbed his large Claymore sword. It was a magnificent example and the ricasso was silver encrusted with rubies and emeralds.

'Well, man, what are you waiting for? Lead the way!'

In his fury he did not bother to cover his bare chest with his shirt. The sentry led the way out of the castle and within five minutes they had reached Greymare Rock.

Chapter 30

Raising the Alarm

Having given the castle a wide berth, Hugh headed towards the coast where his horse could gallop on the firm coastal tracks and sandy beaches towards Newcastle.

The strong-willed beast had not flinched at the thunderstorm that had blown over the coast several hours earlier. Hugh thought he heard the faint sounds of an alarm horn being blown once they reached Craster. He hoped this was not the case and did not share his concerns with Agnes.

An observant castle sentry had spotted Hugh's speeding horse heading south; he shouted orders for a chasing party of fast horses to be ready within minutes. He then ran to the beach to inform Constable Binchester. He also decided to release a pack of lymer hounds which were quickly shown Hugh's horse in the distance and would nosily and eagerly pursue their quarry. Their sound would also offer an audible guide for the castle's horses, which would soon join in the pursuit.

Hugh's mistake of returning to the coast too quickly would cost him dearly over the next two hours.

Criggle was semi-awake, but was still paralytic from the wine he had consumed.

'How...how nice of you...to, to join me...'

He slurred and started to laugh.

The sentry had gone to check on the prisoner.

'Sir! The woman has escaped!'

Criggle was trying to sober up fast, realising he had been tricked. He had clambered to his feet and was now staggering around, vaguely watching a sea otter devouring a fish on a pile of wet barnacle covered rocks. The high tide was only two and a half hours away.

Constable Binchester, now in a rage, raised his sword and swung it full strength at Criggle's head.

'Criggle, you cretinous churl!'

Criggle turned just in time to see the blade swoop down before it cleanly sliced his head off. Blood pumped out of the top of his spine like a pulsating jet flow. The sand in the vicinity turned crimson red. His head flew into the air and when it landed on the beach it rolled several times before stopping. His eyes were still open and there was a drunken grin on his face. A nearby crab started to scuttle over his head.

For good measure, Constable Binchester then rammed his sword into Criggle's torso several times.

Concerned about his career and possible punishment from the earl once he had returned from his current campaign, the constable bellowed at the sentry,

'If you don't want to be next you better find me that whore so I can kill her myself!'

They both ran back to the castle, where they were greeted by the waiting hunting party.

'Sir, the dogs are chasing two people on one horse to the south. We are ready to leave on your command!' He passed the constable a shirt to wear.

'Well done man! At least someone has a brain! We leave at once!'

Chapter 31

Sugar Sands

HUGH's horse passed Sugar Sands and Boulmer beach. By now he could hear the unmistakeable sound of barking hounds in pursuit. What could have woken the guard?

Agnes could sense a problem.

'Are those dogs tracking us, Hugh?'

'Possibly, though if they are we will shortly be approaching Alnmouth bay, where we will be able to cross the deep waters of the mouth of the River Aln. The dogs will lose our scent there.'

'I am scared, Hugh! I cannot swim! What if I fall off the horse? I will drown!'

'Just hold on tight, my darling, you will be fine.'

Agnes, pleased at this term of endearment, briefly forgot her concerns and gripped Hugh's waist a little tighter. The Aln estuary was now in sight.

At the castle, twenty horses had just begun their pursuit. With only one rider to each horse, they had a distinct weight advantage over Hugh and Agnes, and the hounds were making enough noise for the riders to follow without difficulty. Constable Binchester tried to work out who could have freed the prisoner as he led the group of horses in pursuit.

Hugh's horse entered the deep channel of the River Aln. The mare was a veteran swimmer and swam across without hesitation. Hugh could feel Agnes trembling at the sight of the fast water in the now twilight. Hugh made a mental note to teach her to swim if they could make it to a safe destination. If only...

Once they were safely across the river, Hugh's faithful strong horse galloped south towards Warkworth, where they would have to make another crossing at the River Coquet.

Little did Hugh realise that, although the pursing hounds could not smell through deep water, they were able to follow their scent through the air.

Chapter 32

The Crossing

Sensing they were gaining on their quarry, the lymer hounds jumped into the river in unison and quickly reached the southern river bank. Some of them shook their bodies to disperse the water from their fur, but others, driven by pure killer instinct, continued so as not to lose ground.

As the group of pursing horse riders approached the Aln crossing, they had to ride in single file on the sand between the shoreline and Marden Rocks. Numerous fresh pawprints and a set of horse hoofprints were visible in the sand. Several riders at the back who could not swim decided to detour and then cross at the bridge in Hipsburn. They hoped they could catch the group and this act of cowardice would therefore go undetected. All the riders knew the area well.

They were unsure which was worse, the possibility of drowning or the fury of Constable Binchester. They were already aware of the rage-fuelled beheading that had taken place on the beach earlier that night.

Hugh's horse briefly detoured inland to avoid the rocks at Birling Carrs and then re-joined the firm sand in front of the dunes leading into Warkworth. Even with the weight of its two passengers, the well cared-for mare galloped at an incredible speed. They gap between Hugh, Agnes, and their pursuers began to widen.

They had now reached the Coquet crossing. This was more precarious, as the mud flats had to be negotiated to be avoided. Many a rider had made a mistake here, just north of Amble. Daylight was now fading fast but the almost full moon provided plenty of moonlight to help Hugh navigate. He thought, optimistically, that the sound of the pursing hounds was staring to fade. In fact, he thought they would have given up at the Aln crossing and was surprised to hear them at all. Hopefully he would finally lose them at this wider, more treacherous crossing.

As the horse walked towards the estuary just north of Pan Point, it disturbed foul-smelling mud which clung to the hair on its legs. Luckily, it was washed away by the current. This channel was deeper and had a stronger current going out to sea which was counteracted by the incoming tide.

A barn owl flew silently in front of the horse's head, ready to start its night of hunting in the sand dunes, searching for small rodents in the warmth of the summer evening.

Agnes was speechless with fear and gripped Hugh so tightly that he almost winced. After several minutes, the horse's hooves were able to get a purchase on the sandy southern shoreline of the river. On terra firma once again, the horse picked up speed on the firm sandy beach at Druridge Bay below Amble and continued southwards.

The pursuing dogs had now reached the Coquet crossing. They could hear the hunting horns of their masters behind them, goading them to make the crossing and continue. One of the dogs got stuck in the mud in its eagerness; the more it struggled the deeper it sank. Within seconds, all of its legs were firmly trapped. It panted heavily while the others jumped into the water to make the crossing. One of the weaker dogs struggled in the current and was swiftly taken out to sea.

The strongest dogs had now reached the safety of the shore and recommenced their pursuit. There were no more river crossings and Hugh's horse was starting to slow down in the distance, so these dogs would start to close the gap once again.

The horse riders reached the final river crossing as the last dogs crossed the river. One of the riders noticed the hound trapped in the mud. He dismounted his horse and was about to come to the aid of the helpless beast when he heard a shout behind him.

'Leave it! And get back on your horse. We have no time for weakness! Let it be wolf fodder!'

Empathy was not a word that could be used to describe him. In fact, most of these men were brutes, many of whom had not been above using their crop whips if their horses faltered. This had been the case of the two riders who had taken the Hipsburn crossing. Although they had once again caught up with the main party, their mounts were now too exhausted for the river crossing that faced them. These riders knew the bridge crossing detour here was too long, and manoeuvred their horses to the river's edge despite their paralysing fear of drowning. The first horse reared up, not used to deep water, and its rider was tossed into the river. He screamed and splashed around frantically in the deep, cold water. He shouted for help but quickly tired and drowned shortly afterward. The riderless horse turned around and ran on its own northwards along the beach from whence it came.

The other, exhausted and hesitant, moved along the bank only to get stuck in the mud. The angry rider fell off and started to beat the horse, but he also started to sink. Fortunately, the horse managed to free itself from this potential muddy coffin and, as its rear left leg came loose, it kicked its rider square in the face, breaking his nose. Sinew and blood poured into his mouth. He clutched both of his hands to his face, screaming in agony.

Once free, this horse also ran towards the north in a panic. All the other riders had crossed the river by now and, in an eerily silence, the stranded rider looked over to the hound in the mud twenty paces away. In the moonlight, he could see the fear in its eyes. With the ever-approaching tide and the distant sound of wolves howling, his bowels involuntary emptied as he realised that water or beast would soon take his life.

Chapter 33

Distant Sounds

Hugh could feel his mount slowing slightly. Although she was in her prime and enjoyed vigorous exercise, all animals had their endurance limits. Fortunately, both Agnes and Hugh had lithe physiques; any extra weight on the mare would have been disastrous.

Hugh was furious with himself for misjudging his journey timings, guided only by the sun, moon and tide. Had he had freed Agnes later, as he had originally intended, he knew for sure that he would have missed the midnight boat departure at high tide. He looked out to sea and noticed the tide approaching and the first seed of doubt was planted in his mind that they would be captured.

He could once again hear the hounds barking in the distance; it was clear that the gap was closing. Agnes sensed Hugh's tension.

'Hugh, is there something wrong?'

He knew that, if caught, they would face an utterly cruel death. However, rather than alarm her, he simply replied,

'Not at all. Soon we will be approaching a port where a boat is waiting to give us a safe passage away from here.'

She remained unconvinced, but did not ask any more questions for the time being. She looked over her shoulder for the first time but no hounds were visible, despite the distant barking.

Having reached Snab Point, they joined a track lined on both sides by vast swathes of yellow gorse. They soon found themselves beneath a canopy of Scotch pine trees which emitted a pleasant aroma, mixed in with the salty air. Fortunately, there was a bridge over the River Lyne once they were south of Lynemouth. Hugh had a good knowledge of the area and decided to keep west, slightly inland, so he could also use the bridge crossings for the Rivers Wansbeck and Blyth.

Chapter 34

Seeking Revenge

Constable Binchester, who now had the hounds within in his vision, was starting to enjoy the chase. He was thinking of perverse and sadistic ways to kill the fugitive and her saviour. He would take great pleasure in the process, and ensure that his methods were as prolonged and painful as inhumanely possible. It suddenly dawned on him – Agnes's saviour must be the soldier who had stayed at the castle en route to Berwick, and had comforted her when she was questioned. He decided he would let her watch him die first, so she could see what would become of her.

Speaking out loud, he declared,
'No one makes a fool of me. Revenge will be mine! That damn Parrock will suffer!'

Although he was now approaching a part of the coast with which he was not familiar, Constable Binchester knew that the fugitive's horse would soon come to the end of its endurance limit. He also correctly predicted that they were heading for a port to make their escape. What was more, he knew that, although the hounds were slower than horses, they had greater stamina and it would be difficult to stop them once they closed in on their quarry.

Hugh's horse was now galloping inland towards Seaton Delaval. Few people were travelling on this track at this time of night. There was always the risk of highway robbers, but they were to the east of the Great North track, which was popular with raiders, so an attack here would be unlikely. High tide was a little over an hour away. Even in the moonlight he could see the sheen of sweat that had formed on the horse's neck.

The lingering smell of extinguished cooking fires filled their noses as they approached a large area of civilisation. The embers smouldered outside huts whose occupants were now sleeping inside.

Livestock were startled by the fast horse passing by, despite being protected by wicker anti-wolf screens.

'We are nearly at the port!' Hugh shouted to Agnes. 'I have a deal planned with a stable owner not far from the pier to sell my horse before we set sail!'

'She is magnificent. I will be sorry to see her go. What is her name?'

'Dromos. It's Latin for racer.'

'How apt! There are few like her.'

'Aye!'

Hugh heard the faint sound of the church bells ring eleven times as they entered the outskirts of Wallsend. He gently stroked Dromos's mane, thinking to himself that the sounds of the pursuing hounds were definitely getting louder. Although the hounds were fast, they were slowed each time they had to detect fresh scent trails.

Agnes had never travelled this far south.

'What is that in the distance?' She cried in wonder.

'That is what's left of Hadrian's Wall. A gift from our former Roman hosts!'

'It's amazing!'

In this era, it was still magnificent. Although parts of it had been pillaged to construct local churches and cathedrals, much of the seventy-three-mile construction still remained, especially in remote areas.

Before them, a deliberate gap had been made in the wall to allow easy passage through to the river piers on the banks of the Tyne. The wall itself ended a short distance to the east.

Chapter 35

A Sad Loss

THEY passed through the gap in the wall and Hugh rode towards the stables at Walkergate, where he would sell his beloved horse. He hoped the stable keeper wouldn't quibble over Dromos's condition, exhausted as she was.

The Wallsend clock chimed quarter past the hour.

Shortly afterwards, they arrived at a copse. Their entrance startled a bouquet of pheasants – incidentally, another offering from the Roman Empire – which had been roosting in the trees. The birds flew from all directions into the path of the approaching horse.

Alarmed by the sudden onset of the birds, Dromos lurched to the right, straight into the hole of a badger set. She came to a sudden stop, ejecting both Hugh and Agnes into a mud bank covered in ferns which cushioned their fall. They lay stunned on the ground, their nostrils filled with the ferns' pleasant, earthy aroma.

In the chaos of the fall, Hugh had not missed the sickening sound of Dromos's leg breaking. Slightly bruised, Hugh dusted himself off and quickly ran over to his beloved horse, which was panting from pain and exhaustion.

Hugh knew what he had to do and shouted over to Agnes to look away. Tears were welling in his eyes.

Hugh pulled out the dagger which he had taken from Criggle, and started to stroke Dromos's coat gently. Leaving no time for hesitation, he pushed the blade through her skull, killing her instantly and relieving her from her agony. He withdrew the dagger and cleaned the blade. He leaned in close to the horse's ear and said his goodbyes.

'Thank you. Rest in peace.'

Hugh pocketed the dagger and ran over to Agnes. She was in shock from the fall but otherwise uninjured. Hugh grabbed her hand and started to run with her towards the piers – he would no longer be selling Dromos, of course.

He was still grieving for his horse but his overwhelming concern was now the monetary shortfall caused by her death. Although Agnes had her freedom so far, he worried about would happen once they got to London. At least their passage was partly paid in advance, and he still had enough for the balance once they arrived.

Hugh's knowledge of the area was essential – as they ran towards the piers, the church bell chimed to signify the half hour before midnight. Hugh heard the sailors on the Tyne shouting orders to get ready for a departure on the arrival of high tide.

Chapter 36

Geeson Is Discovered

THE hounds had now arrived at Dromos's corpse. In their fury, some of them started to rip open the horse hide with their teeth and devour the bloody meat within. It was most fortunate for the once magnificent horse that she was no longer alive.

The pursuing riders arrived shortly afterwards. Constable Binchester made a cursory check of the area to see if Agnes and Hugh were hiding in the copse. He quickly realised they would have left on foot, so he dragged one of the hounds which were not feasting to the place where Hugh and Agnes would have been sat on the horse.

'Go find!' He ordered the dog.

The hound picked up their scent and started to run towards the piers, quickly followed by several others.

Constable Binchester then commanded to his fellow riders to follow him.

'Come, we will follow on foot! I just hope the hounds leave some sport for us. And let it be clear that neither is to be killed!'

He blew the hunting horn as a taunt.

By now, Hugh and Agnes had arrived at the Tyne piers. Hugh quickly identified the cog they would be sailing on. It was low in the water, laden with its cargo of coal. Over a dozen of these vessels were lined up and loaded, ready to depart in twenty minutes' time. Once the high tide had safely covered the precarious sand banks in the channel, the sailors would row to the mouth of the channel when the sails would be raised. The captain greeted Hugh and Agnes on the pier. They all heard the distinctive sound of a horn in the distance.

'Look, I don't want any trouble. And I guess I'd be right in saying that someone is looking for thee!'

'Do not let it concern you, sir. We can sail now and be gone before they arrive. Here is your other coin.'

'Nay, ladde, on three counts. If we go now we will get stuck on the sand banks and it will look suspicious if I leave before the others!'

'And the third?'

'The price has doubled. Four gold coins for the two of you. Take it or leave it, son!'

Hugh knew it would be pointless to argue. He handed over the balance of the gold coins.

'And another thing: if your friends get here before we leave and they find you on my boat, I will deny everything. You understand?'

'Yes, Captain, as you wish.'

'Right, young woman, you go to the stern of the boat and hide, and pray for high tide!'

'And you, ladde, go below deck and prepare to row with my crew when I give the command!'

They duly did as they were instructed; neither spoke as they boarded the cog and the clock struck a quarter to midnight.

Chapter 37

On the Piers

CONSTABLE Binchester was running fast, following the sound of the barking hounds. He could make out the river piers and cogs in the distance. He grew increasingly confident of a capture as he guessed they would be on one of these vessels. Recalling the damage his hounds had inflicted on the dead horse, he knew there would be little left of the fugitives if the hounds got to them first. He decided to call off the dogs by blowing the horn three times. They were obedient and responsive, having been severely beaten in their training.

The dogs stopped in their tracks and began to whine and bark eagerly, longing for their master to give the command to resume the hunt.

Just a handful of minutes before midnight, the constable stood on the pier and drew his sword as he boarded the first cog. He was angrily confronted by its captain.

'Oi! What d'you think you're doing, man? I'm about to set sail!'

Constable Binchester expertly pointed his sword at the captain's throat, where a small droplet of blood appeared.

'Two fugitives are close by and I am searching your boat, unless of course you object?'

'No, sir, be my guest!'

The constable withdrew his sword before turning around and calling out to his men.

'You three make a thorough search! I will stop the other boats from leaving.'

'Silence!' He shouted at the hounds as he stepped back onto the pier. They whimpered and then calmed into submission as they had received too often the result of their master's displeasure.

He then marched down the oak planking boats to the middle boat.

'Listen, all captains! One of your boats contains two prisoners, one man and one woman. No one is to leave until I say so. Is that clear?'

Various insults were hurled back. These sailors only got paid once their deliveries were made in London and they did not care for strangers giving orders.

'Who are you, the vassal of Newcastle?'

'Clear off! Find your own boat!'

'We don't take orders from strangers!'

Constable Binchester knew sailors were a feisty bunch and the last thing he wanted was a riot. He decided to try a different tactic, one which he knew would make them all compliant.

'Captains, search your boats. The one who finds me my fugitives will be rewarded with two gold coins!'

He wasn't carrying any money but would think of something once they were found. The bells at Wallsend now started to strike midnight, signifying the arrival of high tide.

Chapter 38

Midnight Hour

AGNES was hiding underneath a spare sail in the stern of the boat. She could hear a commotion of dogs barking and a man shouting. Her skin scrawled as she recognised the voice of Constable Binchester. She could not clearly make out what he was saying but she knew it would not be good news. She peered out from underneath the sheet and looked into the dark, uninviting water. She decided she would rather jump in and drown than be recaptured. She knew the alternative would be a gruesome death.

Hugh was below the deck, holding his allocated sea oar near the bow of the cog. The other crewmembers could see the fear in his eyes. He had heard the conversation on the pier. He put his hand on the dagger in his pocket. If soldiers boarded the ship he would take both Agnes's life and his own. He knew perverse punishments would be issued if they were caught, especially to Agnes. The thought made him sick. He heard the church bells strike midnight

All pandemonium broke out as the captains frantically searched their cogs on the promise of a reward. Once they realised the fugitives were not on their boats, and not wanting to miss the high tide, they untied the mooring ropes and gave the order to row out in to the main channel of the Tyne.

Two guards were still searching the end cog as it cast off from its mooring. They panicked once they realised the boat was leaving. One managed to jump on the pier before the gap was too great. The other plunged in to the cold water and was promptly rescued.

Four captains, however, were determined to find the fugitives on their boats and remained moored as their crew ensured that no keg was left unturned.

Hugh's captain gave the order to set sail. The fare Hugh had paid was double the reward. He had been tempted to claim that as well, but decided the risk was too great.

Hugh's fellow oarsmen had all their eyes on him; he took out his purse of coins and placed it on the rowing bench so they could all see it.

'That's all I have left. It's all yours. I beg you to start rowing.'

He hoped these men had compassion and women and family of their own. He was aware of the desperation that must have shown on his face.

'The woman is innocent and, if recaptured, she will be brutally tortured before she is wrongly executed.'

The sailors looked at one another, waiting for someone to make a decision. They also looked at the coins which were bulging in the purse; they guessed this amounted to several months' wages each.

Hugh's heart was pounding fast. Suddenly a sailor gripped his oar and smiled, then they all started to row in unison and the boat slowly reversed out into the main channel.

Chapter 39

A Race Begins

By now, all the cogs had either been searched by their respective captains or by Constable Binchester, who was angry and frustrated that his quarry had slipped away. They had all started to set sail.

He stood on one of the piers, shouting and cursing the men around him.

'Damn them! Now I have lost them!'

One of the sailors on a nearby cog taunted the master of arms.

'Fear not, noble sir! All these fine ships are going henceforth to the port of London. Race you!'

With this he threw human faeces at him. It landed square in his chest. The sailors on board started to laugh and gesticulate.

Incensed, and with his pride severely dented, the constable vented his fury on the nearest hound to him, killing it instantly with his sword. He then turned to his men and shouted,

'One smile, smirk or word of this back at the castle and I will cut off your balls and make you eat them!'

All the men stood solemn-faced, their bowed heads helping to conceal their inner glee. What a great story to tell: that the master of arms had been humiliated by a common sailor.

The constable ripped off his foul-smelling shirt and threw it in the water. He ordered the nearest guard to divest himself of his shirt and give it to him.

The only person on Hugh's cog to witness this incident was the captain. A plan that would earn him the reward of two gold coins started to form in his mind.

Constable Binchester was certain that they were on one of the cogs. They were either being helped or had avoided detection. He now regretted halting the hounds, and to verify if he was correct, he blew the hunting horn for the hounds to resume searching. All the hounds started to bark and ran to the water's edge. They barked wildly, sensing the deep, fast-flowing channel of water below them. At least this confirmed they were on a ship bound for London.

Chapter 40

Home, I Remember Forever

MEANWHILE, the crowd which had gathered at Greymare Rock had dispersed once they had seen the empty handcuffs and decapitated body lying on the beach. They had missed all the entertainment.

On the pier in Newcastle, Constable Binchester gave his instructions.

'You, man!', he shouted, pointing to the first man in the group. 'You will take the hounds back to the castle in the morning. And remember, breathe not a word of this, or else!' He grabbed his own testicles menacingly.

The man gulped.

'Yes, sir!'

'The rest of us will follow the great Roman road south to the Port of London, as a welcome party for the whore and her saviour! We will ride dusk 'til dawn so I suggest you ensure you and the horses are fed and watered. We leave at sunrise!'

Exhausted from the tension of the previous few hours, they all did as they were instructed. None had travelled this far south and did not relish the journey due to the fact that the Earl of Lancaster was opposed to King Edward II, thus putting their lives in danger as men loyal to the King would be searching for traitors.

The cog transporting Hugh and Agnes was approaching the end of the estuary which led into the open North Sea. Hugh and the other sailors rowed in silence. The expression of relief at his narrow escape was all too apparent on Hugh's face.

Agnes was too frightened to move from her hiding place underneath the spare sail until the cog had been at sea for almost half an hour. She could the see the back of the captain as he stood controlling the steering oar located on the starboard side, navigating the cog out to sea. Hugh had not said where they were going, just 'South'. All she knew was that she could trust this kind, handsome man who had saved her life and that she would gladly travel with him wherever he decided to take her.

As the Northumberland coastline started to fade into the distance and the sky was filled with a wonderful green display of the Aurora Borealis, Agnes spoke quietly aloud.

'Hyem I mindin on ay.'

Home, I remember forever.

Part Two
London Bound

Chapter 41

Making Plans

THE cog transporting Hugh and Agnes had now raised its sails, releasing the sailors from their rowing duties. Hugh thanked his fellow sailors once again before excusing himself to seek out Agnes at the stern. He nodded to the captain as he passed him by.

'Hugh! I am so glad to see you again.'

Hugh sat down next to her.

'You may not be so happy to see me,' he replied, 'when I tell you I am now penniless and have no idea what to do when we arrive at the Port of London. I am so sorry, Agnes.'

She squeezed his hand.

'Do not apologise. You have saved my life, and we still have each other.'

After a brief pause, she continued.

'So, our destination is London. I have heard stories of this southern city. What would you have planned if you still had the money?'

'To stay in this country would be dangerous. My plan was to buy us passage on a ship abroad, as far as our coin would have taken us. But without the sale of Dromos, and thanks to the captain's greed and my bribe to the crew, we have nothing. I suppose I will have to think of an alternative. You must be exhausted. Please try to get some rest and we can talk more in the morning.'

Hugh pulled the fabric of the spare sail over them to try and keep warm. Although it had been warm and humid on land, here out at sea it was surprisingly cold.

The skies above were clear and pitch black. No clouds covered the moon, treating the two of them to the most magnificent display of the stars and galaxies above. A shooting star even passed over the horizon.

In time, all the crew were asleep except the solitary sailor working through the night to navigate using a mariner's compass. Hugh had one hand on his dagger just in case. All the crew were now aware he was destitute, at least, so he was not afraid of being robbed.

At sunrise Hugh woke to see a pod of bottlenose dolphins playfully jumping in and out of the water. They had no trouble keeping up with the slow-moving cog, which was only travelling at an average speed of four knots. But this method of speed measurement was in fact almost three centuries away from discovery.

No land could be seen from the starboard side, as the trade cogs would usually stay out to sea to avoid treacherous stretches of rocky shoreline. There were no other ships in view, either – the cogs' varying payloads quickly separated the convoy, but ultimately they would arrive at their final destination within twelve hours of one another. This particular cog would be arriving in three days and seven hours' time from its port of departure, weather permitting.

Chapter 42

In Pursuit

CONSTABLE Binchester awoke at sunrise, refreshed and eager to resume the chase. He noticed that the guard whom he had commissioned to return to the castle with the hounds had already left.

After a brief breakfast of oats and cold rabbit meat, and having tended to the horses, his party of riders left the camp. As the horses were only partially rested after their galloping exertions from the previous night, the constable decided to keep the horses somewhere between a trot and canter. The distance to London was incalculable to him – he only knew that the old Roman road would lead him there and his horses would have a much greater speed advantage. He was painfully aware, however, that his horses would require breaks each day, whereas the boats could travel nonstop. Nonetheless, the element of surprise was on his side.

A race had well and truly begun. All bets would be on the horses, especially as the amount hours they were being ridden each day exceeded their physical limits by the cruel and vindictive determination of their master.

He rode until the heat of midday before making a stop by the side of a stream.

'Ensure the horses are watered and fed before we leave!'

Little did he know that he had already travelled an

impressive forty-two miles, and that by the end of the day he would cover almost ninety-six.

The countryside was relatively flat, and was covered in vast swathes of oak forest. Red squirrels were busily collecting early acorns which had started to fall and bury them in preparation for the winter months ahead.

They passed small settlements of people who had set up home next to this busy trade road. They overtook numerous horses and carts, but encountered none of the robbers they had heard existed. Clearly their large, heavily armed riding party was enough of a deterrent. Just before nightfall, they set up camp just north of the small village of Pontefract.

Many of the riders were suffering from saddle sores, but they did not dare complain, seeing that their master's mood had not improved during the day. Periodically he would shout out to passers-by to enquire how many days' riding it was to London in the south. Many a yokel just looked at him blankly and shrugged their shoulders. One of the soldiers had managed to kill a fox with his bow and arrow and, once the camp fire was alight, the wild dog was promptly skinned and cooked. Its tail was kept as a mascot.

The fox meat was served with watercress from a nearby stream and wood sorrel. Most of the party belched loudly in approval. The soldiers settled down for the night, under the watch of one poor guard who had been told that his tongue would be cut off if he fell asleep. This was incentive enough to stay awake all night, despite his exhaustion. He was offered a brief period of sleep at sunrise while the camp prepared to head south for the second day of their journey.

Chapter 43

A Captain Contemplates

ON board the cog, the captain was pondering the conversation he had heard as they left the pier.

Would the irate horse rider really pursue the boats, having been told that they were all heading for London? Having convinced himself that, yes, he would, the captain resolved to talk to his crew as they approached London and discuss their options. Perhaps he could claim their bounty after all.

Hordes of sea birds were tracking the cog, but they quickly lost interest once they realised it was not a fishing boat and no scraps of food were being tossed overboard.

The food on board consisted of dried fish and meats that would not perish, accompanied by oats and warm-tasting water. However, the basic food was still more nutritious than that which Agnes had received during her incarceration.

Agnes and Hugh spent much of the day watching the passing birds and dolphins. They could make out the shapes of two more boats from the convoy against the horizon. They were comfortable in each other's company. In his presence, Agnes relived the happy days with her mother and the agony of never meeting her father. In turn, Hugh recounted the loss of his beloved mother. He described the shame that his desertion would bring on his family, although, as he said, he had never been enthusiastic about being in the military and was not a man of violence. He was sure he would not be missed.

Both Hugh and Agnes had a strong Christian faith and said a prayer for the loss of their loved ones. They did not realise it yet, but they were starting to fall in love.

As their boat started to approach Cromer, it made an easterly turn. These sailors were experienced and had travelled this route numerous times.

At the back of Hugh's mind was what he would do once they reached London. But at least, he thought, they were not being pursed anymore...

Chapter 44

Brief Respite

In no time at all, the horse riders reached the town of Homestead on the Rother, or modern-day Rotherham. One thing they noticed as they travelled south was the variations in their native tongue. Throughout the country, people's speech differed depending on the area in which they lived; these variations had developed between the Norman Conquest in 1066 and the late fifteenth century.

A rest was provided after this twenty-seven-mile journey. The horses drank water from the River Don while some of the soldiers caught salmon from the river. The river was teaming with fish and the salmon were easily caught by spearing the fish with their arrows.

Constable Binchester flagged down the next man he met at the river.

'Can you tell me how many days we are from London?'

'It's right far. Maybe tomorrow or the day after – depends if you ride like a girl or man!'

The constable was not in the mood to trade insults and gave the order to leave. As they rode through the town, lavish preparations were being made for a large banquet. He decided to make a stop here on his return journey and hoped that Agnes would be sharing his bed for the night. He would then pass her to his men before killing her. His mood improved, and his group sensed this change too.

After another day's hard riding, they stopped for the night at the town of Peterborough and camped next to the River Nene. After speaking to a local, it was determined that with one more days riding it would be possible to reach their destination. The day's ride had lamed one of the horses, and its rider was duly instructed to kill it so they could feast on horse meat that evening.

The solider wondered how he would travel without a horse.

'Looks like you have a long walk home, you son of a strumpet!' Constable Binchester cackled. 'Head east to the sea and then north, you canker blossom, I really could not care! Now piss off, out of my sight!'

After an evening's feast and rest, Constable Binchester was eager to depart the next morning.

'To London we ride! You horrible urchins better pray we get there today.'

With this, they left the camp. The lone horseless soldier started to walk eastwards with a satchel crammed full of horse meat, not knowing if he would ever see his wife and family again.

By early afternoon they had reached Biggleswade. The locals here confirmed that London could be reached by the end of the day, so once the horses were watered they were encouraged to trot faster. The land was becoming increasingly populated, and by nightfall the strong scent of cooking fires filled the air.

Before midnight, they had reached the outskirts of England's largest and wealthiest city. They were pointed in the direction of the river Thames, where the Port of London was waiting. Within twenty minutes, the river was in sight. This port was huge compared with Newcastle's. Large barque ships were moored along the piers.

Constable Binchester instructed two guards to wait on a patch of grassland where there was stabling and an inn. Although he did not have the two gold coins he had falsely promised as a reward, he did have sufficient low denomination coins to pay for expenses from the castle coffers. These were securely hidden in a leather purse in his clothing. He gave a few coins to his men so that they could pay.

Ignoring all the warehouses of wool, wine, pottery and other fine wares, the constable strode along the pier with the other guards in tow. At Newcastle when he had searched the cogs he had found them laden with coal. Now all he needed to do was find the correct unloading pier.

He spoke to one of his men and instructed him to find and track the whereabouts of the sailor who had thrown excrement at him and then report back. He would deal with him later.

Being outside of his jurisdiction, and with growing tensions between the earl and the king, he was taking an incredible risk. His plan was to hide along the dockside with his men spread out at intervals, hidden out of sight. As soon as Agnes and her companion were on dry land they would swiftly detain them and be on their way. He was confident they would not evade him this time. They were early – there was a large empty space on the dock side where the flotilla would arrive the next morning on the high tide. He settled down for the night, knowing that the commotion of the unloading would wake him.

Chapter 45

Double Cross

On the night before the cogs would start to arrive in London, the captain of the fugitives' ship decided to share his plan with his crew.

'Men, I have thought of a plan whereby we can claim the bounty for our passengers' heads. I will trick the man into a false sense of security by saying I have a guilty conscience, as I overheard his pursuers being informed that we are London-bound and that they would be there waiting on our arrival. To seal his trust, I will give him back a gold coin and tell them to jump overboard as we approach the Thames and to lay low for a week until his pursuers give up. Of course, what will really happen is that I will speak to the man in charge when we land and I will tell him we only discovered them on board this morning and, once found, they jumped overboard and swam to shore. I will also inform him that they stole your wages. As the fugitives will have been instructed to wait, their search party will find them quickly and easily, enabling us to be paid the reward and have my gold cold returned!'

'Captain, you crafty ol' sea dog! Count us in!'

'That's settled then. Let's try to get some rest. We will take turns at the steering oar. I will wake them at sunrise and when we reach the Thames estuary I will convince them to jump.'

At just before sunrise the next morning, the captain duly woke Hugh and repeated his story. Once he had placed a single gold coin in his hand, Hugh believed him wholeheartedly and thanked him for the warning.

'I cannot land you, mind. There are too many treacherous sand banks. I will get you as close as I can to the shore at East Tilbury Marshes. You won't have to swim far to shore and the current will not be strong. I will let you know when to jump.'

'Thank you, Captain. I cannot thank you enough.'

The captain had a sudden pang of guilt. If Hugh only knew the truth.

Hugh woke Agnes and explained what was going to happen.

'But Hugh, I cannot swim! I will drown!'

'Agnes, listen to me carefully. I will not let anything happen to you. When we jump into the water it will be cold. The current will not be strong. You must not panic or you will pull me under the water. I will guide you to the shore. I repeat, you must not panic, and we will be fine.'

'I promise I will not panic. I trust you.'

Shortly afterwards, the captain informed Hugh that it was time for them to jump. He had used the steering oar to get within forty feet of the bank, which meant an easy swim to shore. Hugh held Agnes's hand and they jumped together into the cold waters of the Thames estuary.

Chapter 46

A Trap Awaits

THE pursuers waiting at London docks had a peaceful night in their hiding places. Once the boats had left on the high tide the previous evening, the area remained quiet throughout the night. Fortunately, there were no local guards protecting the area; Constable Binchester would have found it hard to explain their situation. Once awake, he and his men ate a breakfast of dried barley.

The first cog from the Newcastle convoy arrived shortly after sunrise. Once its ropes were secure on the pier, unloading of its cargo began. No unexpected passengers disembarked, nor did this cog contain the crew member who had humiliated him. The second cog arrived thirty minutes later, but was again of no interest.

Within an hour, the cog containing the crew member he sought revenge on arrived. As per his instruction, one of the constable's guards discreetly started to tail him.

As Hugh and Agnes hit the surface of the water neither was prepared for how cold it was. They both plunged under the surface and Hugh pulled Agnes's hand so that they both resurfaced at the same time. Agnes was panting and spat out the cold sea water. Hugh gently turned her around so she was on her back, then he started to pull her towards the shore. Although it was travelling slowly, the cog was already in the distance.

Agnes had done exactly as she was instructed and did not panic. The water was calm and clear; Hugh could see the sandy bottom of the estuary which was only about eight feet deep. Within a few minutes the water was shallow enough for both of them to stand up. They had reached the periphery of the marsh and could feel the mud underfoot. There were numerous channels leading into the sea as they approached dry land and they could hear the deep boom of a nearby bittern calling. They disturbed a marsh harrier which was devouring its prey and the startled bird took flight, heading inland. The area was covered in a vast array of vegetation including sea oxeye, marsh elder, glasswort and samphire. Having reached the safety of dry land, they moved to an area screened by vegetation to dry off in the strengthening morning sun. To protect Agnes's modesty and embarrassment, Hugh suggested they dry themselves in separate areas, but within earshot of one another, and then rest for a while.

Thirty minutes later, the cog which had transported Hugh and Agnes arrived at the unloading pier. The captain was disappointed that the man offering the reward was not waiting to board and search his boat. He hoped the man had been delayed and would be arriving later that day.

With only seven cogs left to arrive, Constable Binchester was starting to get more anxious. He knew he could not blow his cover, so he waited impatiently along with his men.

By early evening the last cog had arrived, but the fugitive and her saviour still did not materialise from within. Panic now started to set in. Had the cogs stopped en route, or had the fugitives not even left Newcastle in the first place? Had the hounds somehow failed to read a correct scent?

In any case, he had made a dangerous and unnecessary journey. The only consolation was that he would kill the sailor who had humiliated him before he returned home to Dunstanburgh Castle. He quickly ascertained the sailor's current whereabouts and stealthily made his way there. He had left his sword with one of his men – a small dagger would suffice.

The sailor had been drinking at an inn all afternoon, and was the first one to return to the boat leaving his fellow crew to continue their enjoyment.

Constable Binchester climbed aboard in the last minutes of daylight. He was nimble and did not make a sound. He could hear snoring and moved slowly towards this location. Rather than just kill him, he wanted him to know who his assailant was and cause him as much pain as possible. Now he was positioned behind the sailor, he grabbed him in a headlock and covered his mouth with his other hand so he would not be able to shout for assistance. The sailor was much smaller than the constable, and too intoxicated to put up much resistance. Nevertheless, he began to struggle as the constable's arm tightened itself around his neck.

Constable Binchester spoke softly into his ear.

'Remember me, you little shit thrower? I took up your challenge to race you here and it looks like I won. No one humiliates me and gets away with it. I just wanted you to know that before I slice your throat and let you bleed to death.'

On hearing this, the sailor froze in fear. He was utterly amazed that this man had travelled all this way. The sailor was trying to mumble that he was sorry, but the powerful hand covering his mouth made this almost impossible.

Fearing for his life, he started to flail his arms. Constable Binchester stood up and rammed the sailor to the side of the cog so his head was leaning over the sea. With a swift, well-practised movement, the constable reached for his hidden dagger and sliced the soldier's throat, just enough for him to bleed to death but not kill him instantly. Blood dripped into the Thames. He was then lifted and pushed into the river. Once in the water, the sailor grabbed his own throat with one hand to try and stop the bleeding and his waved frantically in the air with the other as the current carried him away. No one had witnessed this incident and there was no evidence of a struggle or blood on the cog. When his crew mates returned later that night, they would assume he was lying in a drunken stupor somewhere nearby and would leave without him. A sailor not returning for their duties was a common occurrence and he would simply be replaced once they returned to Newcastle.

Chapter 47

The Marshes

Hugh and Agnes had been snoozing for several hours now in the warmth of the summer heat. Agnes had chosen a shaded area near some undergrowth, still sunburnt from her ordeal at Greymare Rock. By now her clothes were dry and she got dressed. Hugh heard movement nearby and guessed this was Agnes waking up. He too got dressed and called out to her.

'You must be hungry? I will find us some lunch.'

'Aye, I am hungry.'

Hugh had noticed the vast amount of rabbit warrens in the area but he did not have the required materials to build a snare. He remembered where they had come ashore and decided to go back there and scan for mussels. He had often enjoyed a meal of them along with bread back home in Newcastle – these bivalve molluscs were abundant in and around the River Tyne. There were few pollutants in the water, so they provided a nutritious meal which could be served either cooked or raw.

Once he had arrived at the water's edge, he rolled up his trousers and waded through the mud flats looking for mussels. The tide had now receded. Flocks of feeding wader birds flew into the air as he approached. Hugh managed to collect a large pile within minutes and took them back to where Agnes was waiting. He then scanned the area and collected handfuls of samphire and wild sorrel. One of the more useful things the military had taught Hugh was how to survive by foraging for food. He then cut two pieces of bark off a nearby tree with his dagger – he would serve the food on these. He then opened a dozen of the mussels, placed a quantity of samphire and sorrel on top and passed it to Agnes.

'Enjoy! After we have eaten I will collect some blackberries for us.'

Agnes eagerly ate her meal while Hugh was preparing his own. Once she had finished, she thanked him and offered to help collect the berries. After they had eaten, Hugh started to build a shelter for them in the undergrowth, away from any prying eyes on board ships heading to and from the Thames. The shelter was constructed from upright supports using branches which he either snapped or cut from trees and then covered these supports with reeds. This marshy area was remote and there was no evidence of human civilisation as far as the eye could see.

Although he did not share his concerns with Agnes, Hugh was starting to doubt the cog captains' intentions. Was he genuine or had he set a trap? He did decide, however, that it would be best to wait a few days before they headed to London. They would move further west along the marsh just in case the captain did decide to return. He would not tell Agnes the reason for the move as her journey had been traumatic enough already. He was just glad that she had decided to travel with him.

That night they both slept soundly in separate corners of the shelter he had made.

Chapter 48

No Show

The cog captain that had transported Hugh and Agnes waited all day while the coal was unloaded. He then headed for a local inn with all but one of his crew members, whom he had instructed to keep watch in case the pursuing horse riders should arrive. He would have to return to Newcastle the following day and was starting to regret giving Hugh a gold coin back as the captain's double cross plan had not worked so far. The captain's crew began to spend some of the money they had received from Hugh. In fact, within several return trips all of the money would be spent on frivolities such as women, drink or gambling with dice.

The following morning, they all returned to their cog to find the unloading of coal had been completed. Once the lookout on board had confirmed that no one had come to search for the two fugitives and no search party had arrived on the dockside, the captain realised his plan to double-cross Hugh had failed. Once the tides were suitable for sailing, he would join his flotilla of cogs, set off north to Newcastle and reload with more coal. He did contemplate trying to land his boat near the marshes in an attempt to reclaim the gold coin from Hugh, but realised his boat could get stuck, or worse, damaged. As it was, he and his crew were not fighting men and he knew Hugh's desperation would make him a dangerous man. Instead, he just muttered to himself.

'Aye, lad, you have made a lucky escape.'
He gave his crew the order to depart.
'Prepare to leave and head home on the tide!'
'Aye, captain!'

Chapter 49

Rotherham Beckons

Now that Constable Binchester had sought his revenge on the sailor that had humiliated him, he realised that it was time to head north. He was sure that the King's spies would have noticed by now that strangers with different accents were in the area. He mounted his horse and started to head north with his men. They rode at a much slower pace, giving the constable time to ponder on the excuse he could give for his prisoner's escape.

As per his original plan, he decided that he would make a stop at Rotherham. Here he would blend in among one of the banquets and try to forget his problems. He knew that the network of spies and messengers during these dark times would mean that it would not be long before the Earl of Lancaster got to hear about his failures. His men sensed a change in his mood – none had been reprimanded or badly treated on their return journey. The men suspected that he was trying to win their favour.

After three days of gentle riding, they reached Rotherham and attended banquet as planned. Even vast amounts of wine could not help the constable forget his problems. He also noticed that two of his horse riders had disappeared and prayed that they had not rushed ahead to Dunstanburgh Castle to inform them of his failures, although he suspected this was the case. He considered disappearing himself, but as he had little money he decided to head north in the morning. A demotion was the best he could hope for.

Within a week, they arrived back at the castle. Waiting at the gates to welcome him were four guards, accompanied by John de Lilburn. He would prove to be so efficient that the following year, in 1323, he would be appointed the new constable of the castle and a new tower bearing his name would be constructed in his honour.

'Robert de Binchester', John de Lilburn announced, 'I hereby arrest thee for allowing a prisoner to escape from her punishment of drowning and for your gross dereliction of duty in using castle resources to travel to London and back. By the authority given to me, I hereby sentence you to receive the same punishment at high tide tomorrow evening. Guards, take him away!'

Constable Binchester thought about begging for mercy, but he knew this futile attempt would only further add to his humiliation. As he was unceremoniously dragged away, his head was filled with one incredulous thought: how could a lowly kitchen maid have got the better of him? Once in his cell, he was given a last supper of slop which the castle pigs would have struggled to eat. He had a crazy notion, during his last night, that perhaps one of his men would show some loyalty and try to rescue him. Before he fell asleep for the last time in his life, he thought perhaps it would have been better to have not returned to the castle – to have lived the rest of his life as a pauper instead. He would never know. The constable dreamed that night of all the wrongs he had committed during his life and prayed for forgiveness. Not even his God could save him now. His dreams were interrupted by footsteps approaching his cell shortly after dawn.

Chapter 50

Fall From Grace

His cell door was abruptly opened and he was taken outside by four guards, who had also travelled with him from London to Greymare Rock. As they approached the rock, human remains, which must have been Criggle's, came into view. Two weeks had passed since he had been slain and nature's recyclers – wolves, foxes, seagulls and crabs, to name but a few – had devoured every inch of flesh on the corpse. The guards were enjoying their task.

'Well, Binchester, looks like you'll be joining Criggle today!'

They chained the former constable to Greymare Rock once the tide had started to go back out. Strict instructions had been given that a dozen guards were to remain here all day, just in case he tried to escape. The high tide would return at early evening.

Several hours before the tide was starting to return, a large crowd gathered to witness the drowning. John de Lilburn was one of the first to arrive.

'I, John De Lilburn, hereby sentence you, Robert de Binchester, to death by drowning. Have you any last words?'

With defiance in his eyes, Binchester spat at the new constable.

'I demand to see the Earl! This is preposterous!'

'Oh! Haven't you heard? Your beloved Earl has been captured; no one can save you or him now.'

This was true – the earl had been defeated at the Battle of Boroughbridge, and his later execution would end the long period of antagonism between the king and the Earl of Lancaster, thus enabling Edward to re-establish his authority and remain in power for a further five years. Some of the guards were uncertain as to what this would mean for them and thought 'better the devil you know', but none had voiced this or even tried to help Constable Binchester. By the next day he would be a distant memory.

One hour before high tide, local people had started to arrive and a few of the braver ones who had witnessed the prisoner's wrath started to throw rotten vegetables at him. The constable's body was covered from head to toe in a multi-coloured, foul-smelling paste, and he eventually vomited all down his front. Shortly after this, a drunken man appeared in front of him.

'Remember me? You forced me to walk home after making me kill me horse! Took me eight days! You told me to piss off and that I will do!'

He turned to walk away. A desperate Binchester, a man who had been stripped of his rank and, soon, his life, called back in a frantic tone.

'Wait! I am sorry, my friend. Help me please! I am a rich man, free me and all my money is yours!'

The guard ignored him. He climbed above the rock and shouted over the crowd.

'Fellow friends, would you like to hear my ode to a toad?'
'Yes!'
'There was a constable called Binchester, who couldn't even drown a spinster! He has now lost his crown and will

soon drown! This is a sight I don't want to miss…so I give you this!'

With this he started to urinate all over the constable's head. The crowd responded with raucous laughter.

The guard's hot urine poured over the constable's face and mixed in with the smell of rotten vegetables. Other guards who had travelled to London started to torment him, too.

'Hey Binchester, it's a shame your shit-throwing friend couldn't make it today!'

The tide now reached his toes and the creeping cold water made him struggle against his chains in a state of desperation. The metal cut into his wrists and ankles, his blood mixing with the cold water.

'Let me go! I order you all to set me free!'

The crowd just laughed, realising that he was minutes away from drowning. The tide had now reached his shins. Even in the summer heat the sea water was extremely cold. Another large wave covered his body, temporarily submerging him in the cold sea water.

By now he was in a state of complete panic as the tide had now reached his chest. The crowd enjoyed his suffering.

He tried to tilt his head back to allow himself to breathe through his nose. Shortly afterwards the tide left him completely submerged. He could make out the silhouettes of people on the surface pointing and waving at him as he drowned. Within a couple of minutes, he lost consciousness and fell limp.

His corpse was removed at low tide. The crowd had long ago dispersed and returned to the castle. The new castle constable had left instructions for Criggle's burial at the church in Embleton. He also requested that the skeletal remains of Criggle be removed and disposed of accordingly.

Life returned to normal under the watchful eye of the new castle constable, the previous one all but a distant memory...

Chapter 51

No More Waiting

Hugh awoke early and refreshed the next day and gently woke Agnes from where she was sleeping. She had already made a remarkable recovery from her injuries.

'I'm afraid it is mussels and samphire for breakfast, again.'

Agnes thanked him for the food and was quietly glad to be moving on today. They could not live the rest of their lives here at the marshes – in the winter it would be a hostile place.

Today they would start their journey westward to the Port of London. After breakfast they walked together in the early morning sun.

Hugh had decided to stay close to the bank of the Thames because, although the cog captain had assured him it was less than two days walking to the port, Hugh was unfamiliar with the area and was unsure as to what they would encounter on the way.

Within a couple of hours, they came across the first signs of civilisation. Strangers were obviously commonplace and no one paid them much attention. Their arrival would have attracted attention in the tight-knit communities along the remote Northumberland coast.

People were going about their daily business in the glorious weather. By early evening, Hugh decided to stop and camp for the night. During the day all they had eaten was wild berries that they had collected for the journey from Tilbury marshes, and they were both hungry. But Hugh only had one gold coin and he knew innkeepers would be unlikely to have the required coinage in change. What was more, he was still unsure of their ultimate destination once they reached London. He and Agnes chatted gaily along the route, which was a welcome distraction from his worries.

Chapter 52

Aromas

HUGH and Agnes arrived in London in the mid-afternoon, under another glorious summer sun. The city was larger and busier than that of Hugh's home city of Newcastle. The buildings seemed bigger in size and of a slightly different design. Most dwellings had smoke dispersing from the chimney stacks from the cooking pots. The air was filled with a glorious aroma from the variety of dishes being cooked. Agnes did not want to become separated from Hugh in the ever-increasing horde of people and stayed as close as possible to his side.

'So, Hugh, what is our plan?'

'We will go down to the river and find lodgings for the night. And in the morning we'll check out the piers and see where the vessels are bound for.'

Hugh had heard stories of large trade ships leaving London for mysterious far-off places. He knew certain ones had to be avoided due to war and conflict, and he would be sure to make an allied country their destination. What he had not shared with Agnes was how they would pay for the fare. He could run the risk of living in the south, but as they had strange northern accents people would be suspicious of them. Although he doubted Constable Binchester would continue to pursue them, he did not want to live his life constantly looking over his shoulder. Therefore, their only safe option would be to flee abroad and start a new life. Perhaps they could stow away on board? A captain would not turn back if they were discovered, but how would they survive? They were risking starvation, arrest on arrival, or worse, being thrown overboard.

He would try to solve this quandary the next day, once they had arrived at the piers.

Within a short while, they could smell the salty tidal waters of the north bank of the Thames. There was also a pungent smell of human effluent, which had been deposited in man-made trenches before flowing into the river. There was a wake of red kites soaring above in thermal heat of the summer evening; these magnificent birds with a wing span of up to six feet were excellent scavengers looking for any suitable morsels left behind by the residents of the city. They were, in fact, more orange in appearance than red, however the descriptive colour orange did not yet exist.

There were several large trade cogs moored at one of the many piers. The boats moored there were much larger than the coal cog they had used to travel from Newcastle.

'Hugh, these ships are magnificent!'

'Aye, they are surely that. Let's find an inn for the night. We can enquire as to their destinations in the morning.'

They entered the first inn that they came to. Groups of men sat around tables in the large open space beyond the door, talking loudly, laughing, drinking and gambling with dice. Hugh and Agnes were approached by the owner of the inn.

'Can I help you?'

'Er, yes please,' Hugh responded. 'Have you accommodation and food for us?'

'Yes, you and your wife can have my last room. It will be three groats per night each, payable in advance. And another groat if you have a horse.'

Hugh, clearly embarrassed that the innkeeper had assumed they were married, turned red in the face. He paused and was about decline the offer when Agnes spoke.

'Perfect – thank you. We'll take the room. Oh, and we have no horse.'

She leant over to Hugh and whispered into his ear.

'We don't want to arouse suspicion. If the constable has spies here they won't be looking for a married couple, and you can sleep on the floor.'

'You're right.' Hugh said, and turned back towards the innkeeper. 'Yes, we will take the room. Have you change for this coin?'

The innkeeper's eyes lit up at the sight of the gold. He raised it to his mouth and bit down on it, hard.

'Don't see many of these around 'ere. Just checking it were a real 'un.'

He then produced a quantity of groats from his purse and gave Hugh his change.

'Follow me. I will show you to your room.'

Hugh and Agnes followed the innkeeper up a narrow staircase which led to a small room; the innkeeper opened the door for them. As they had started to climb the stairs, two of the men gambling with the dice nodded at one another.

'When you are settled I will serve you mutton and pottage along with my finest ale.'

Hugh thanked him and closed the door once he had gone. This small but functional room had a window made up of panes of flattened animal horn, which looked out over nearby buildings. Hugh opened the window and took in the sounds of the hustle and bustle from the street below.

'Agnes, I don't know about you, but I am famished.'

'Aye, Hugh. Let's eat!'

As they had no possessions to unpack they headed straight back down to the main bar area. The innkeeper greeted them as soon as they crossed the threshold.

'Your mutton and pottage is on the stove in the corner. Would you like a tankard of ale each?'

'Aye, that would be great.'

The innkeeper served them their ale, which they sipped while walking over to the stove. The two men who had shown an interest in Hugh and Agnes earlier both got up and walked towards them. Hugh and Agnes were chatting away about their plans for the next day. They had decided to walk down to the piers first thing and see where the ships were heading. Hugh had only paid for one night's accommodation and knew the number of groats still in his possession would not get them far.

One of the two men had also moved towards the stove to wait for his meal.

'You ain't from these parts are ya? Perhaps you and your missus would like to join me and me mate for a game of dice?'

'We are fine, thank you.' Hugh replied, nervously. 'We don't gamble.'

The other man, pretending to be more drunk than he actually was, stumbled and brushed past Hugh.

'Beggin' your pardon. Sorry.'

Hugh moved to the side and replied.

'That's fine.'

Hugh and Agnes had not realised that the stumbling man had taken the opportunity to pocket Hugh's bag of money. The two robbers returned to their table, ate their meal noisily, and then left the inn shortly afterwards.

Having not eaten a cooked meal since leaving Newcastle, Hugh and Agnes ate their food enthusiastically. Neither was a big drinker, so the ale had made them feel both light headed. After second helpings for each of them, Hugh and Agnes retired to their room. They were both tired from the two-day walk to London. They wished each other a good night and, having said their prayers in silence, Hugh curled up on the floor and Agnes fell asleep almost instantly on the bed.

Chapter 53

The Helper

They both woke refreshed in the morning and eagerly made their way downstairs for breakfast. The city was already a hive of activity, with market traders setting out their wares for sale and people tending to their animals or small businesses.

As Hugh and Agnes entered the main bar area, they could smell a fresh aroma of bread and porridge. The innkeeper appeared.

'Morning. Help yourselves to breakfast. Will you be wanting another night?'

'I'm afraid not. We have to be on our way today.'

'As you wish.'

The innkeeper returned to his other guests and left Hugh and Agnes to eat their breakfast.

'Agnes, once we have eaten we will be on our way. We need to be alert, just in case we have been followed.'

'Aye, Hugh. I am excited, but nervous at the same time. Who knows where we will end up? But wherever this journey takes us, I am just glad it is with you.'

They smiled at one another and ate the remainder of their breakfast in silence. Once they had finished, they thanked the innkeeper and left for the short walk down to the docks. The walk was pleasant underneath the warm summer sky.

Having arrived at the docks, both Hugh and Agnes stood in awe at the scale of activity. People were shouting orders for the ships to be loaded or unloaded. Numerous porters were carrying goods ranging from wool and food to metals and coal. Hugh had also underestimated the number soldiers guarding the port. With the high level of security, it seemed unlikely that they would be able to stow away on a ship.

'These ships look magnificent, Hugh! I wonder where they are all travelling to?'

'As we know, the coal cogs are from Newcastle. Of the others I am unsure. They are European – so perhaps France, Spain or even Portugal. I am not sure how far our money will take us but we will soon find out.'

Hugh smiled and then patted the place where he had hidden the bag of coins in his clothing. His hand could not detect it and he frantically started to search his clothing but to of no avail. Tears started to well up in his eyes.

'Hugh, what is wrong?' Agnes said with concern.

'Agnes, I was such a fool to think that I could save you. We are now here, penniless and on the run with nowhere to go. Perhaps if I return to Newcastle alone and take your punishment it will be enough to secure your freedom. You need to stay away from me! All I bring you is bad luck.'

'Nonsense, Hugh, I will not leave you. You saved my life and you are the kindest person I know. You have risked your life too! We are in this together.'

Hugh raised his voice in a tone far harsher than he had intended.

'Don't be foolish, woman. You must go now – all I have brought you is bad luck. I am sorry but it is for the best!'

Agnes started to sob, great tears running down her cheeks. This had alerted the more chivalrous men in the vicinity.

'Is this fella bothering you, miss? Do you need help?'

'Oh no, it's fine. Thank you.'

The man stood tall and glared at Hugh in a manner that said he was lucky he had not intervened further.

A captain of one of the largest ships at the docks had overheard most of the conversation. He was extravagantly dressed in a large captain's hat and a long coat with a large metal buckle adorning the belt around his middle. His shoes were also of a fine quality.

'Excuse me, please let me introduce myself. I am Captain Tudor Felstead of the Isolde and I may be able to help you.'

Agnes stopped crying and Hugh eyed him suspiciously, suspecting this was some sort of trap.

'And why, kind sir, would you help us?'

'Forgive me; I overheard some of your conversation. I suspect you have been the victim of one of this fine city's low-life pickpockets. To show that we are decent people, can I offer you and your wife safe passage on my ship?'

'She is not my wife and why would you offer a free passage?'

Hugh had gently taken Agnes by the elbow and was trying to guide her away from the area.

'My dear fellow, my apologies for referring to this young woman as your wife. The passage on my ship would not be for free. One of my crew members has been taken ill and I require a galley hand on board. And perhaps you, young man, could assist with my cargo?'

Agnes eyes lit up and a smile began to spread across her face.

'Hugh! How wonderful, but a different kind of kitchen to the castle.'

Hugh looked at Agnes sharply, thinking that she had revealed too much information. He did not trust the captain.

'Thank you, kind sir, but we really must be on our way.'

With this he started to pull a reluctant Agnes away from the pier.

'Wait! Look, I know it must look strange me inviting you on my ship but I really am short of crew. We're leaving tonight and are bound for Tavira in Portugal. Have a think about my offer. If you change your mind, the Isolde will be sailing from the docks at high tide. You can't miss her – she is the largest ship there. If you give me your names I can let the guards know to let you on board.'

'Er, Charles and Constance. Thank you. We will think about your offer. Good day, sir.'

With this Hugh dragged Agnes away into the crowd.

'Hugh, why did you lie about our names?'

'We cannot trust anyone, Agnes. If he were a spy looking for fugitives he will already know that you worked in a kitchen castle. I suspect he will order our arrest. We must leave now and hide!'

Chapter 54

The Wager

THE captain had lied – he was not looking for additional crew. His true intentions would be revealed if Hugh and Agnes were to board the Isolde. He had left instructions with his crew for them to be escorted to his cabin should they arrive. This was not the first time he had taken fugitives on board. He was a philanthropist and tried to help people in need when he could. Up to now no one had ever passed his rigorous tests of character. Captain Felstead was an orphan who had started working on ships at an early age and slowly, over the years, had worked and saved hard to achieve a captaincy on board the Isolde. This magnificent ship was used a trading vessel for wine between Tavira in Portugal's Algarve and the Port of London.

Portugal's good relationship with Britain dated back to the twelfth century when the English crusaders had assisted Portugal during the Reconquista.

Captain Felstead gave his orders in preparation for the ships departure. All the wine he had brought back from Tavira had been unloaded and the goods, including wool and tin, were currently being loaded on board for sale on their return. Soon it would be ready to leave on the high tide, and the captain wondered if Charles and Constance would accept his offer. He doubted very much that they had given their real names. The captain's second in command knocked on his cabin door.

'Enter!'

'Hello, sir. The loading of the ship and supplies is almost complete and we will be ready to sail on the high tide.'

'Thank you, Golding. Have any extra passengers arrived?'

'No, sir, are we to expect more waifs and strays?'

This was an insubordinate comment, however Golding was a loyal and long-serving employee of the captain and would only jest in his private company – not in front of the men. He was well-aware of the captain's views on humanity and found them rather humbling.

'I have invited a man and woman on board. Shall we apply our usual wager?'

'Yes, Captain. One bottle of Portugal's finest wine it is!'

On the previous six or so occasions he had wagered this bet, the captain had lost. As with the others he hoped the two he had met today would be different, assuming they even turned up.

Chapter 55

The Offer

Hugh and Agnes walked in silence along the banks of the Thames. It was now lunchtime and their hungry stomachs were rumbling. Strong aromas of food being cooked and sold to passers-by only accentuated their hunger. Agnes walked by a trader who was selling a stew of potato and mutton.

'Oh, Hugh, if only we had money to purchase some food!'
'Aye, I am famished.' Hugh replied.
He approached the vendor.
'Have you any work, so we can earn some food?'
He looked at Agnes with lecherous eyes. The man was old and wrinkled with most of his front teeth missing.
'I am sure I could spare ye some food if she were nice to me. Real nice, that is!'
With this comment, they both moved swiftly moved away from the area. Once away from the trader, Agnes turned to face Hugh.
'Let's be honest with one another, Hugh. We have to accept the offer from the captain we met earlier. We cannot continue like this – we have no money or food.'
'But what if it is a trap? You would face a punishment far more severe than drowning. People do not just offer journeys on board ships!'
'You heard the man. He said he was short of a galley hand so we would have to earn our keep.'

Hugh paused, reflecting.

'This is what we will do. I will go to the captain and you will wait on the dock side. I will confess all to test his integrity. If you do not see me come back onto the deck and wave a piece of material then it is has been a trap, although quite what you would do after that I don't know.'

An awkward silence followed. With her beautiful looks Agnes could easily find someone to help her, but at what cost?

'If you insist, Hugh. I suppose we have no other choice.'

They walked along the dockside and it wasn't long before they spotted the Isolde. She was a magnificent merchant ship with three sails capable of transporting large quantities of goods. She was a Crayer design, weighing over fifty tonnes, and they were largely used for cross-channel trade. She was even armed with two small cannons for protection on board. Since the discovery of gunpowder by the Chinese, advancements had been made in weapons that fired projectiles.

'Agnes, you must wait here and keep out of sight. Look up at the deck. If, as agreed, you do not see my signal then, then... good luck.'

Before she could respond Hugh had already started walking to the dock side. Before he could walk more than a few feet, he was confronted by a guard.

'Wait! What is your business here?'

'My name is Hugh, I mean Charles...Captain Felstead is expecting me.'

'Well, Hugh, or Charles, or whatever your name is, wait here until I return.'

Hugh was angry with himself for revealing his name before he had spoken with the captain.

Five minutes later the guard returned.

'Follow me.' He announced sharply.

Hugh dutifully followed the guard on board the Isolde. He was impressed by the sheer size of her. Porters were busily loading the remainder of the goods on board in preparation for departure. Cured meats, salted herring and pickled eels and barrels of water were also being loaded for the long journey ahead. In the vast food store were numerous foodstuffs which, during the journey, would provide sustenance for the onboard rat population.

The guard approached the captain's quarters and knocked on the door.

Chapter 56

Meeting the Captain

A voice responded from within.

'Enter!'

The guard opened the door and indicated for Hugh to go inside. Hugh had consciously laid his hand on the knife hidden inside his clothing but knew he would not be able to put up much of a fight against these seafaring men. Hugh entered the impressive quarters of the captain, who nodded to the guard as he closed the door.

Hugh looked around the room and could see a tin plate of pickled meats and bread on a large wooden desk. This started his stomach rumbling again.

'Charles, how nice of you to come. I take it Constance will be joining us?'

'Captain, both you and I know they are not our real names. Can I be honest with you?'

'Of course. Please take a seat and help yourself to some food.'

Hugh drew up a wooden chair as instructed and quickly ate one of the bread rolls. Once he had finished he looked at the captain sitting opposite.

'Sir, the young woman's name is Agnes and mine is Hugh. She was wrongly convicted of murder, I helped her to escape on the day she was sentenced to drown and I have deserted the army. We managed to secure passage here on a coal cog but I have since lost all my money, which was needed to buy us safe passage out of the country. If you are to have me arrested I beg you spare Agnes's life.'

'I see. And what makes you think I will have you arrested?'

'Why else? I have bought Agnes nothing but bad luck since freeing her, the least I can do is offer myself as a sacrifice to save her.'

Hugh, you and I are not that different. I try to help people too. Today you were fortunate to find me, that's all. My offer of travel still stands in return for your employment on board. I appreciate your honesty and realise how brave it was of you to reveal the truth.'

Hugh sat there for a moment contemplating whether it was some sort of trap. He could see that the captain was a rich man so doubted that he would be motivated by any monetary reward. After a short while, Hugh appeared to have made up his mind.

'Have you a piece of cloth I can borrow, please?'

'A strange request, but yes. See one of my men on the deck. Will you both be joining me for the journey?'

'Aye, yes we shall. I will return soon.'

Hugh left the cabin and entered the deck area of the ship, where he was approached by one of the deck hands.

'Can I help you?'

'Aye, have you some cloth I can borrow?'

The man looked at Hugh oddly and passed him a sail patch. Hugh then walked up to the port side and waved the material for several minutes.

Chapter 57

Passage Secured

Agnes had been waiting on the dockside. She didn't know if she would ever see Hugh again, but prayed that she would. She was famished and thirst scratched at her throat as she stood in the midday heat. There was so much activity with the street traders and loading and unloading of the ships, that no one had paid any particular attention to her. Her eyes were firmly fixed on the port side of the deck of the Isolde. The wait was agonising. She knew the ship would be leaving soon and time was running out for both of them. Casting around for distractions, she admired the size of the ship. The sail masts were high; clearly the tallest of oak trees had been used in her construction. She sat low in the water, laden down as she was with cargo. The name of the ship, painted in gold, glinted in the sunlight.

Her heart skipped a beat when she saw Hugh appear on deck. Seeing him wave a piece of material, Agnes was unable to contain her excitement and ran towards the Isolde. As she approached she was stopped by a guard.

'Stop! State your name and business.'

Hugh was watching as Agnes approached and shouted down to the guard.

'Please let her pass! Captain Felstead is expecting her.'

The guard hesitated, clearly not used to taking orders from anyone other than the captain. By this time, the captain had heard the shouting and left his cabin to investigate. He looked down to see that Agnes was being obstructed by one of his guards.

'Ward! Please let the young woman pass.'

'Aye, Captain, as you wish.'

Agnes climbed aboard the Isolde and was greeted by a rather excited Hugh.

'I am so glad to see you again, Agnes! It seems my faith in humanity has been restored. The captain assures us we can earn a safe passage to Portugal.'

'I am so glad to be going with you, Hugh. I am nervous though – I've lived all my life in Northumberland.'

'It will be a new life and an adventure for us both!'

This was to be their second journey via the sea in a matter of weeks. The One Hundred Years' War was some way off and, although the War of Saint-Sardos was only around the corner, the only potential problems en route would be the weather and pirates...

Part Three

Portugal Bound

Chapter 58

The Isolde

THE Isolde left as scheduled at high tide, along with all the vessels that were ready for departure. The Isolde was the only ship travelling to Portugal – the others were destined for France. It would take just under ten days to reach their destination, almost twelve hundred nautical miles away. She made slow progress until she reached the English Channel where the winds were much stronger, allowing her pace to quicken.

As the only woman on board, Agnes was given her own small cabin. Hugh was to sleep in a communal area with the male crew. Agnes was shown her duties in the galley – a cramped area where she would prepare the meals for all the crew three times a day

On the second day, Hugh was sent for by the captain.

'I take it you and your travel companion are both comfortable on board?'

'Yes, thank you. You have been most generous.'

'I have called you here to help me with some errands. The men are becoming restless because I have not paid them for their last journey. My crew of ten are each owed five silver farthings. I want you to go and pay them from this purse, then return the empty purse to me. After that, you can help me work on the ship's inventory.'

The captain handed Hugh a purse containing silver

farthings. What he didn't tell him was that he had deliberately put fifty-five coins inside, rather than fifty.

Hugh left the cabin with the purse and dutifully did as he was instructed. Once he had completed the task, he realised that five silver farthings still remained in the purse. He was slightly surprised, knowing that educated men would rarely make such a mistake, but returned it to the captain's cabin nevertheless. What Hugh did not yet realise was that this simple act of honesty would eventually make him an extremely wealthy man.

Hugh handed the captain the purse containing five silver farthings. The captain was pleased that Hugh had passed his test, and looked forward to claiming his winnings from Golding.

The next day, working with Hugh in his cabin, the captain struck up an unexpected conversation.

'Hugh, have you given any thought to what you will do once you arrive in Tavira?'

Very little, rather foolishly, I fear. I suppose we would live in exile, and I would look for work for both of us.'

'Although Portugal is our ally, there are still spies there for the king. It's unlikely, but you may be questioned on arrival and it will look suspicious if you arrive as an unmarried couple. As a sea captain I can perform the ceremony on board. You will also need to learn Portuguese. Golding can help you with this. I suggest you and Agnes start lessons as soon as we are finished here.'

Although there was no doubt that Hugh was falling in love with Agnes, he had not been contemplating marriage so soon.

Chapter 59

The Proposal

HUGH went to find Agnes, who cleaning the galley after lunch had been served. She was enjoying her new role on board, especially as there were no cruel males overseeing her work.

'Agnes, I need to talk to you about when we arrive in Portugal.'

'Yes, Hugh, what is it?'

'I – I've been talking to the captain and he – he says that we should...'

'What is it, Hugh? What's wrong?'

Hugh stood there, unsure of how to ask her to marry him. Instead, when the ship moved downwards he took Agnes in his arms and kissed her passionately. She was surprised at this sudden move but did not resist his advances and responded by kissing him back.

After a few minutes they both broke from the embrace. Hugh quickly asked the question, unsure of what the answer would be.

'Agnes – I loved you from the first moment we met. Will you marry me?'

'Oh, Hugh, I love you too! Of course I will marry you!'

They returned to the captain together, and Hugh asked for them to be married.

'Hugh and Agnes, many congratulations. I would be only

too pleased to marry you, but only when you can ask me in Portuguese. Go, find Golding and start your lessons now!'

Hugh and Agnes left to search for the captain's second in command. He sat them down and started their first lesson in Portuguese.

'From now on we will only speak in your new language. Olá!'

Hugh and Agnes looked at one another and laughed. They were both quick learners and by the fifth day they were able to hold basic conversations in Portuguese.

One day, a pod of dolphins interrupted their lesson jumping in and out of the water in front of the bow of the ship.

'Golfinho!', they both exclaimed.

With their new-found knowledge of Portuguese they had given one another names. Hugh called Agnes his angel, 'Serafim', and Agnes called Hugh her little saint, 'Santos'.

In the distance, the faint outline of another ship could be seen. This was the first one they had seen since leaving London, and they were now midway through their journey. Although Golding has lost his bet to the captain, he had warmed to Hugh and Agnes and was impressed by how quick they were learning.

'Rápido! Vai buscar o Capitão que temos companhia!'

Hugh ran to the captain and relayed the message.

Now at Golding's side, the captain enquired about the mystery ship on the horizon. His conversation was in Portuguese and Hugh and Agnes tried to follow it the best they could.

One of the words alarmed Agnes. 'Pirata'.

Chapter 60

Ceremony at Sea

THE unfamiliar ship was slowly closing the gap. It was smaller than the Isolde, but also lighter and more agile. The Isolde was heavily laden with goods, which made it more sluggish in the water.

By noon the ship was clearly visible and appeared to have set out on a collision course with the Isolde. Pirate ships contained cruel crews and would show no mercy, especially not to women.

The captain took Hugh to one side and spoke quietly in his ear.

'Hugh, the Isolde has cannons which I will fire once the ship is in range. They will be hoping for an easy bounty and will not be expecting a fight. If they manage to overwhelm our ship you must kill Agnes quickly. Pirates will show her no mercy. Do you understand?'

'Yes.'

'Keep her hidden under deck until this is over.'

Hugh guided Agnes to her quarters, trying to remain jovial.

'Hugh, I am not stupid. I am well aware of what would happen should they board his ship. Do not fret, my darling, I will not let them take me. Please be careful.'

She kissed him on the cheek as he left.

Now back on deck, Hugh could see the pirates waving their swords and shouting.

'Abandon et personne ne vont être lésés!'

'What are they saying?' Hugh asked Golding. 'I don't recognise the language.'

'They are French. They're telling us if we surrender no one will be harmed. But they're lying – if they take the ship they will kill us all.'

The captain was busy instructing his men to prepare the cannons. Most cargo ships did not have the luxury of them and usually fell foul to pirate attacks. He had paid a small fortune to have them on board but had already proved their worth on several occasions

The pirate ship was now on the starboard side and within firing range. The captain gave the command.

'Fire!'

There was a plume of white smoke as the cannon was ignited. At such a short range, the cannonball could not have failed to hit its target and tore a hole into the fore deck of the pirate ship.

The captain had given the order for the second cannon to be fired. This time it missed and there was massive white spray of water as the cannonball harmlessly hit the surface of the water. By now the first cannon had been reloaded and was now ready for firing. Once again, the order was given to fire and this time the cannonball smashed into the lower deck. The pirate ship was beginning to sink. The crew on board were hysterical. The few that could swim had jumped overboard and were swimming towards the Isolde.

The captain then gave his next order.

'Archers, fire at will! No man is to board our ship.'

Cries of mercy in both French and English could be heard from the water.

The three sailors were excellent marksmen and, at such a short range, could not fail to hit their targets. One of the arrows had hit a pirate in the shoulder and he was screaming in agony. The surface of the sea had turned red as his blood flowed from the wound.

Now the pirate ship was on fire and all the remaining men had jumped into the water – even the ones who could not swim. In the distance the first dorsal fin of a blue shark could be seen approaching. Although these sharks rarely attacked live humans they would not pass up the opportunity to feed on the flesh of a corpse. Some of the pirates had spotted the shark in the distance and screamed with renewed cries for mercy.

The captain looked down on the surface of the sea where twenty or so desperate souls were pleading for their lives. He knew he could not rescue them as they were no better than the rats that had stowed away on his ship. He would only have to turn his back for a moment and they would slit his throat and take command of his ship.

With a feeling of guilt heavy in his heart, the captain watched this sorry group of humanity in the sea as the Isolde continued to sail by.

Chapter 61

The Rename

The next day at sea was to prove equally challenging. Hugh had intended to ask the captain to marry them, but his plan was foiled by the swathe of storm clouds that had started to form on the horizon. The bright blue sky had turned a dark grey colour, and the gale-force wind whipped the water up into large waves.

The captain gave the order to lower the sails and batten down the hatches. Agnes and others on board had started to pray silently for a safe passage to their destination. She was fortunate enough to not have witnessed the recent incident with the pirates but Hugh had relayed some of the details to her.

They were talking about their new life ahead in Portugal when a large wave crashed into the starboard side of the Isolde. She violently pitched to one side, knocking them both off balance. Hugh's head crashed against the bulkhead and grazed the skin above his left eye.

Agnes rushed to his side.

'Hugh, are you alright?'

'Aye, it's just a graze. A storm must be on the way. Stay here below deck. I will find the captain and see if he needs any assistance.'

Before Agnes could protest he had left. Six of the crew were desperately trying to lower the sails as they could be torn away at any time. Hugh found Golding and the captain assisting the other crew members. By now it was raining so hard that he had to shout to be heard.

'Captain! How can I help?'

'Help the men rig the storm sail!'

Hugh duly did as he was instructed. The ship was becoming more controlled in the storm now that the main sail had been lowered, but she continued to tilt at precarious angles and there were a few times when all on board were convinced she was about to capsize. Each time, fortunately, she levelled herself. At one point the captain had contemplated throwing some of the goods he was transporting overboard to make her sit higher in the water, but as the storm started to abate, this measure remained unnecessary.

They entered calmer waters the following day. The temperature on board was increasing as they were now approaching the Mediterranean Sea. Some of the crew were already showing signs of scurvy as they had not stopped in London. This mysterious illness abated once sailors were on dry land and their vitamin C intake increased.

Hugh went to find the captain and made his request.

'Capitão a vontade você por favor nos casar!'

'Yes, Hugh, I will gladly perform a marriage service for you. God and Golding will be witness to this. Go and fetch Agnes.'

Hugh went to find Agnes in the galley, excited that to make this beautiful woman his wife. They returned to the captain's cabin, where he and Golding were already waiting for them. The captain presided over a simple, Christian service.

The captain then produced a ring from his pocket. It was gold with a green stone set in the top. The ring was exquisite and the craftsmanship was of the highest quality.

'Hugh, this is a ring for your new wife. I can't remember where or when I acquired it during my travels, but it deserves to be worn.'

He passed it to Hugh who then placed it on Agnes's finger. The ring fitted perfectly. Tears welled in her eyes.

'Thank you – it is so beautiful! I will treasure it always.'

'You are most welcome.'

The captain went on.

'We land in a few days. As a precaution, I recommend that you change your surname and also say that this is your second visit to Portugal. That way you should remain safe. Is there a particular name you would like?'

Hugh and Agnes smiled and announced their new name together.

'Yes, Serafim-Santos.'

'As you wish! Serafim-Santos it is. Golding's wedding gift to you both is the use of his cabin until we dock.'

Chapter 62

Land Approaches

WHEN Golding was alone with the captain he smiled and declared:

'No doubt they will be fornicating under the consent of the King tonight!'

The captain smiled knowingly. He himself had never married although he had numerous liaisons over the years in different ports. He was married to his work. He felt an almost paternal affection towards Hugh and hoped to remain friends once they had docked.

Hugh and Agnes were nervous spending their first night together as neither had been intimate before. That night, however, they consummated their marriage and would later find out that Agnes had become pregnant with their first child. The next day, Hugh and Agnes stood on the foredeck looking at the coastline that would soon become their new home. The cloudless sky was an azure blue and a sea breeze cooled the air.

By lunchtime the port of Tavira was in view with numerous whitewashed buildings gleaming under the midday sun. The captain sent for Hugh and Agnes shortly before they docked.

'Hugh and Agnes Serafim-Santos – I just wanted to wish you both a happy life here in Portugal. When you first boarded the ship, I set Hugh an honesty test. I had deliberately put too many coins in the purse and you are the first person to pass such a test. As a result of this act of honesty, and as a wedding gift from myself, I hereby give you the sum of five thousand dinheiros.'

The captain tapped his finger on a wooden chest sat on his desk. It was made from beech wood and was covered in beautiful carvings of galloping horses. Hugh had no idea of the monetary worth of the coins but he was overwhelmed by this generosity.

'I... I am so grateful, sir. Your generosity is beyond words. Thank you so much.'

'The box contains two hundred and fifty soldos and twenty soldos are worth a libra. This is the currency you will need. When you arrive, I will introduce you to my contact in the area. His name is Afonso Lopes. He is a good man whom I trust. As you know, I mainly import the wines produced here back to England. Who knows perhaps one day I will be able to purchase yours should you decide to set up such a venture.'

Hugh and Agnes both realised this was a subtle request and it was something they would both enthusiastically embrace. They would indeed remain firm friends with the captain and his crew.

Chapter 63

A New Aquaintance

THE Isolde was now docked at the port of Tavira and the task of unloading her cargo was underway. The captain, Golding, Hugh, and Agnes had all disembarked and had gone off in search for Afonso Lopes. There were few Portuguese sentries in the area and they paid them little attention as their conversation was all in the native tongue.

The captain had warned Agnes and Hugh only to speak in Portuguese – this would help them further improve their language skills in time.

Agnes was not used to the intense heat and would soon learn that seasons did not exist here; snow and cold weather would soon become a distant memory.

They found Afonso in one of his favourite inns. He had spotted the Isolde in the distance as she approached the port and sat outside the tavern drinking red wine and eating fresh olives. Afonso was a large man with a kind face. His skin was tanned from the Mediterranean sun and he was one of the wealthiest wine producers and landowners in the area.

The captain of the Isolde shook hands with Afonso before introducing Hugh and Agnes.

Afonso spoke so fast they could not understand him at first, but Hugh and Agnes understood some of his greeting after he repeated it more slowly.

Fruits, nuts and fish were brought to the table. Some of these exquisite foods Hugh and Agnes had never seen or tasted before, and figs became a particular favourite of theirs.

The conversation was limited due to their basic understanding of the language, but shortly after lunch it turned to business. Afonso was willing to sell Hugh and Agnes five acres of land and a rustic, basic dwelling for half of their money. In addition, he would offer to mentor them on wine production.

The Algarve offered the perfect climate for growing vines. Grapes thrived in a climate that was never too hot, never too cold, and they were guaranteed more than three thousand hours of sunshine every year. The remainder of the couple's money would be used to rent a small house and purchase the vines they required to start their business.

Captain Felstead and Golding said their goodbyes and returned to the Isolde, onto which Afonso's wines were already being loaded. They were to sail back to London in two days' time. A cargo ship not transporting was one that was not earning money.

Chapter 64

A New Residence

AFONSO walked with Hugh and Agnes to their accommodation. It was a simple, one-roomed single-storey dwelling. The walls were whitewashed to reflect the intensity of the sun's heat, and next to the building was a well that provided cool, fresh water for the dwellings in the vicinity. Their new home had one small window with a shutter and the front door was made of solid wood. Inside there was a stove for cooking, two wooden chairs and a bed. The room was filled with the sound of cicadas that were outside. Hugh and Agnes thanked Afonso and they slept soundly in their new marital home that night.

Agnes woke with thirst early the next morning. Not wanting to disturb Hugh, she quietly got out of bed and opened the front door. The sun was powerful and intense even at this early hour. As she approached the well, she could hear a rustling sound in the nearby undergrowth. She was not overly alarmed and proceeded to lower the wooden barrel down the shaft. The sound in the undergrowth became louder and moments later a creature appeared in front of her. This strange-looking animal had long pointed ears and a large mane. Agnes thought it was some sort of devil creature and she started to scream.

Hugh was awoken by the noise. He checked the bed next to him and Agnes was not there. Alarmed, he jumped out of bed and ran outside. His first thought was that she had been recaptured and was about to be killed. He could see Agnes trembling next to the well. He ran to her and reassuringly took her in his arms.

'What frightens you, my darling?'

'A devil creature was here. I thought it was going to kill me but when I screamed it ran away!'

Agnes's screams had alerted their new neighbours, who had also come outside to investigate. After their introductions in their limited Portuguese, Agnes described the creature she had seen with the pointed ears. Some of the locals started to laugh.

'Gato de lince! Gato de lince!'

Hugh and Agnes did not understand the words but as the locals were laughing they guessed it was nothing to worry about. Although lynx were once native to the United Kingdom, they had been hunted to extinction over six centuries before Hugh and Agnes were even born. Nevertheless, they remained abundant elsewhere in the world.

Hugh and Agnes were talking to their new neighbours when another approached with a puppy in their arms. It was a Portuguese Podengo bitch. The neighbour said it would make a good guard dog: it was large and its smooth coat was of the traditional variety, dating back to the fifth century. It was wagging its tail and Agnes took an instant liking to the dog. She thanked her neighbour for the puppy.

'I will name her Invencível, invincible!'

The neighbours were kind to Hugh and Agnes, bringing them small gifts of almonds and olives, and over the next few weeks they enabled them to settle in their new home and improve their language skills.

Afonso helped Hugh to prepare his land for the new grape vines. These would not bear sufficient fruit for at least three years, during which time Afonso would employ Hugh on his own vineyard. Working on the land was physically hard, especially in the heat, and during the hottest parts of the day all work would stop and they would sit in the shade chatting idly.

On one such day Hugh went to find Agnes. She had been vomiting that morning. She had thought it had been caused by something she had eaten, but it was her first bout of morning sickness.

Hugh entered the house where she was resting.

'My darling, do you remember when we swam ashore at the marshes in London and I promised to teach you to swim? Well, that time is now.'

Agnes was about to protest due to her fear of the water but as she trusted Hugh wholeheartedly, she followed him the short distance to the beach. They found a secluded alcove and they entered the surprisingly warm water together, naked. The sandy bottom was clearly visible and small fish swam among their feet. Hugh gradually encouraged Agnes to move into deeper water. A natural swimmer, Agnes's confidence grew within a few short hours.

They spent the rest of the day here and made love on the beach in the fading light.

In the following weeks, Agnes felt a kicking sensation in her stomach. Not wanting to alarm Hugh, she spoke to one of her female neighbours.

'Bebê!' She exclaimed.

Agnes all but ran back to Hugh, overwhelmed by excitement.

'Hugh, I am having your baby!'

'Oh, Agnes, you have made me so happy! I love you so much.'

Chapter 65

New Addition

THEIR firstborn child was a healthy boy. They named him Baltasar, after the biblical king. Life was proving good for the young family, who found themselves welcomed and accepted in the community and the local church. Hugh and Agnes worked hard to manage their own land, and Hugh's wine-making skills continued to improve. Occasionally Captain Felstead would visit on his travels to sample their wine and sit drinking outside under the hot sun.

Slowly, their personal wealth started to increase and Hugh decided to purchase two purebred Lusitano horses for both Agnes and he to ride. He often thought about his horse, Dromos, and missed riding. He was keen to once again feel the exhilaration of speed and the close connection between man and beast. Agnes had initial reservations about the work involved in looking after the two fillies, but soon adored her gift. Her horse was the slightly smaller of the two and decided to call her Sky, reflecting the colour of her eyes. Hugh called his horse Lily, as her eyes were the colour of water lily pads found in nearby ponds. Now with a young son, a dog and two horses, there was never a quiet moment in the household.

Although Agnes was content with her life, and deeply in love with Hugh, she longed for the rugged coastline of Northumberland. At times, she found the weather oppressive and missed the variations of seasons. However, she knew they could never return home and didn't trouble Hugh with how she was feeling, not wanting to appear ungrateful for all that he had done for her. On one rare occasion when they had talked about her escape she did tell Hugh the words she had spoken when the coastline of Northumberland was no longer visible.

What she did not realise is that Hugh also missed Northumberland. On the occasions that Captain Felstead visited, out of Agnes's earshot, he would often enquire about England and ask whether enough time had passed for he and Agnes go back. Each time Captain Felstead gave the same answer: it will never be safe for you. Never return.

At the beginning of their third year in Tavira, Agnes fell pregnant again with their second child. This was also the year that Hugh and Agnes were ready to produce their first batch of wine. Hugh had employed some of his neighbours to help pick the grapes, and longed for the necessary weather conditions.

Fortunately, on the day of harvest, the weather was perfect. Once collected, the grapes were sorted and any rotten removed ones along with the leaves. The remaining grapes were then placed into a large wooden fermentation vessel and all those involved climbed inside bare foot and began to enthusiastically tread them down whilst laughing. Even Baltasar was involved, much to his delight. Thereafter, the mix was stirred by hand several times a day to assist the fermentation process.

Hugh had already purchased wooden barrels for storing the wine. Once they had been filled, the barrel outlets would be stopped with a cork plug made from the *quercus suber* trees that grew in the Algarve. Hugh had also been instructed to fill pot jugs so that the wine could be tested.

The first batch of wine was a great success and, as promised, Captain Felstead purchased all the barrels they produced. With their handsome profit, Hugh made the shrewd decision to purchase more land from Afonso, who was keen to mentor Hugh and Agnes as his own family were not interested in the wine-making business.

Hugh and Agnes named their second child Andrea after their neighbour. Agnes would often tell their children of a strange land many miles away across the ocean where cold flakes would fall out of the sky and turn the landscape white and skies that turned green with flickering shapes during the night.

Agnes often looked to the north, dreaming of her home. The family lived a contented, joyful life until one fateful day over a decade later.

Chapter 66

The Alcove

LYING in bed one bright summer's morning after a restless night's sleep, Agnes decided to get up and go swimming in her favourite cove. As she left their house she looked back on her beloved husband, Hugh, and their two children, who were sleeping soundly. Hugh and Agnes often went for early morning swims together, but on this particular day she decided not to wake him. She went to the horse's stable and then rode Sky through the eucalyptus tree forest, the pleasant, leafy smell filling her lungs. The horse was startled by a group of pond terrapins warming themselves in the morning sun, but Agnes calmed her and they continued on without incident.

On her arrival at the cove, Agnes dismounted and let Sky chew grass next to a small freshwater stream that led into the sea. She then took off her clothes and walked in to the sea until the water was up to her neck. On this particular morning, the water was especially calm, and she swam with confidence further out to sea than she normally would.

Hugh awoke to find that Agnes was not by his side; this was not unusual as she often awoke before him. He spoke to Andrea and Baltasar and said that he was going for an early morning horse ride with their mother. Although still young, they were growing up fast and would be occupied with learning the family business while their parents were out. Hugh went to his horse, Lily, and rode leisurely along the coast towards their favourite cove.

The sea was incredibly calm, and Agnes was floating on her back with her eyes closed, basking in the morning sun. However, she remained oblivious to the slowly approaching danger that had darkened the surface of the water. Here the water was over twenty feet deep and the sandy bottom could be clearly seen. A group of loggerhead turtles were approaching the area, eager to start feeding, and small shoals of multi-coloured fish were swimming close to the surface of the water.

Hugh had now arrived at the top of the cliff and looked down onto their favourite cove. He could see Agnes's mount lazily chewing grass close to the beach, and initially missed the shape of Agnes's body as his eyes scanned the crystal clear water in the bay.

Agnes was startled by something brushing against her foot, then felt numerous stings pierce both her legs. She screamed in agony. She flipped herself upright in the water and started waving her arms above her head.

Hugh was about to ride down to the cove when he heard a scream. He shielded the sun from his eyes with his hand and looked further out to sea, where he could see the faint outline of Agnes waving at him.

Agnes's legs and body had been stung dozens of times by the Portuguese man o' war. These marine invertebrates, named after an eighteenth-century armed sailing ship, are found in the waters of the Algarve were sometimes in groups over one thousand. Their tentacles were typically thirty feet in length but were sometimes up to one hundred. In the fourteenth century some described them as sea monsters, their venomous tentacles capable of delivering painful, sometimes fatal, stings.

Chapter 67

The Griever

Nearby, the loggerhead turtles had started to feed on the jellyfish. They would feast for the next few hours until the tidal waters dispersed their quarry.

Agnes was now struggling to swim, and kept slipping underneath the surface. She was in despair, unaware that Hugh was nearby.

Hugh was now aware that something was wrong. Although Agnes had become a proficient swimmer, he knew she was in trouble and commanded his mount to race down to the beach, where he dismounted before the horse had stopped. He ran to the water's edge and dived into the warm sea.

'Agnes, my darling, I am coming!'

Hugh swam with all his strength to the place where he had last seen Agnes in the water.

The pain in Agnes's legs had become unbearable and she started to feel lightheaded. She started to hallucinate, imagining that she was back at Greymare Rock. The last vision in her mind before she fell unconscious was that of her beloved Hugh and their two children.

She had rolled over in the water, her face underneath the surface. The remainder of the passing shoal of jellyfish periodically stung her lifeless body as they passed.

Hugh was swimming frantically and could now see Agnes floating on the surface of the water. He imagined that she had been attacked by a shark or had a severe case of cramp. He reached Agnes in only a few minutes. He quickly turned her body over and was initially relieved to see her intact, with no evidence of blood. His heart sank, though, when he saw her lifeless beautiful green eyes staring back at him. He knew instantly that she was dead and let out a guttural roar of grief.

Hugh started to swim on his back with his right arm scooped underneath Agnes's left shoulder. It took him over ten minutes to return to the beach. He lay her body down carefully and noticed the red whip-like welts that had started to form on her legs. He sat there, holding her body, for over an hour before two local fishermen came onto the beach. Such was his shock that that he did not acknowledge their offer of help; he just sat there, gently rocking her body as he stared out to sea. The two fishermen retreated from the beach and went to find a local priest. They all retuned forty minutes later to find Hugh in the same position. The priest whispered to the fishermen to wait nearby before kneeling down next to Hugh and speaking softly.

'Forgive my interruption. I can see that you are grieving. Is the woman your wife?'

'Yes, Father.' Hugh responded in barely more than a whisper. 'She was the love of my life.'

'I know your loss must be difficult to accept but we cannot leave her here. She must be buried forthwith.'

'No! Not here. Although my wife never complained of our life here I know how much see missed our beloved Northumberland in England. I must return her there for a Christian burial!'

The priest knew he would have to choose his words delicately. He gently placed a hand on Hugh's shoulder.

'My son, such an act would require a long journey, one which would, perhaps, be unsuitable for your wife.'

There was a heavy pause.

'Father, I have heard of an ancient civilisation called the Egyptians who would embalm their dead in preparation for the afterlife.'

The priest was surprised by this response and was unsure how to reply.

'Father, please help me return my wife to her homeland.'

After a pause, he added,

'I will make a donation to the church to cover any expenses.'

The priest was familiar with embalming techniques used to delay the process of decay during the period between death and burial. During this era, however, such a procedure was usually reserved for royalty, nobles or catholic dignitaries. Hugh sensed that the priest would require further persuasion.

'Father, God has provided me a good living. You can be sure that my donation would reflect what your help would mean to me.'

This was enough to persuade the priest to help. He beckoned the two fishermen over to them.

'I need you to return to Tavira and fetch the town physicker along with a horse and carriage. Tell him Father Ferraz needs help. Take the two horses here and hurry!'

The two fishermen ran to Hugh and Agnes' horses and galloped towards the town. Hugh and the priest sat without speaking until Hugh broke the silence.

'It is ironic that the sea took her in the end.'

The priest, unaware of the significance of this comment, just nodded. While the priest was looking away Hugh discreetly removed Agnes's wedding ring and placed it inside his pocket for safekeeping. After all, he did not know how much he could trust him.

Chapter 68

A Difficult Conversation

Hugh knew he had a difficult conservation ahead of him with Baltasar and Andrea. He would have to return to England with Agnes body for her burial – this was a task he could not entrust to anyone but himself. They would be distraught at losing their beloved mother and Hugh's dangerous journey would take him away for several months. The year was now 1337, and the One Hundred Years' War had begun to rage across Europe. Finding a captain willing to sail the English Channel to avoid conflict with the French would be costly and potentially fatal.

Several hours later the town physicker arrived along with the two fishermen. The priest and the physicker were talking out of Hugh's earshot and he guessed that they were discussing what fee they should charge. He was certain that some of the money would be paid to the church and the rest would be split between the two of them. They came to join Hugh a short while later.

'My son, this is the town physicker who will prepare your wife for the journey back to England. We must take her body to Tavira immediately so he can begin. Then there is the delicate matter of his fee. I have managed to negotiate the sum of duzentas libras, which includes the church donation you mentioned.'

Hugh thought that the sum of two hundred coins was extortionate but he was in no position to barter, and in any case his love for Agnes was priceless.

'Sim, Father. We will visit my house on the way so I can collect your money.'

Hugh did not fail to notice the smile on the priest's face as he announced this.

The priest beckoned over the two fishermen who, knowing that they would be rewarded for their services, were all too eager to help. The priest instructed them to gently lift Agnes on to the cart and cover her body with blankets.

The priest then discreetly paid them a few coins for their efforts. They were pleased as they could now go to the local taverns for a day of joviality.

The three of them rode in silence towards Hugh's house. The physicker was a tall, gaunt-looking man of few words, no doubt suited to this type of work. Just over an hour later they arrived. Baltasar and Andrea came running towards the carriage when they released Hugh was on board.

'Pai! Where is mãe?'

'Go inside, please. I will explain soon.'

Hugh climbed down from the carriage and stepped into their house. He entered his bedroom and removed a small wooden chest which contained his money from its hiding place. The coins were stored in bags of one hundred. He removed two bags from the chest and returned it to its hiding place before going outside and giving the two bags of coins to the priest.

'Father, I need to speak to my children about what has happened to their mother. Will you inform me, please, when my wife has been prepared for travel?'

'Sim.'

The priest nodded at the physicker and they set off towards Tavira.

Hugh went into the house, where he found Baltasar and Andrea waiting for him.

'Sit down, please. I have some bad news.'

'Where is mãe?'

'My darlings, your mother is in heaven.'

Tears started to pour down their cheeks. Baltasar was trying to be brave by biting his trembling lip and gripping his sister's hand, Andrea started to wail. Hugh put his arms around both of them.

'I know this is difficult for you both, but I will need you to stay with Afonso while I bury your mother. Remember all the stories she used to tell you about when she was a child?'

They both nodded.

'I need to return to England to bury her there. I will only be gone a few months.'

'But pai,' Andrea replied. 'Can we come with you?'

'No! It is too dangerous. You can never travel there, ever!'

Andrea was too upset to protest.

Hugh spent the rest of the afternoon consoling his children. Once they were asleep, he made the short walk to his friend Afonso's house.

Afonso was sitting alone outside his substantial house in the fading light of the evening. He saw his friend approach and knew immediately that something was wrong. Hugh relayed the events of the day and was not ashamed to cry in front of another man.

'Afonso, you are my closest friend here. I'm afraid I have something to ask of you at this difficult time.'

'Sim, anything.'

'I need to return to England to give Agnes a Christian burial in her beloved homeland. Will you look after Baltasar and Andrea while I am gone?'

'Hugh, are you crazy? There is a war. And what if you are captured in England? I know the dangerous circumstances that brought you here.'

Hugh had once divulged his story to Afonso, having guessed that, in any case, Captain Felstead had probably told him.

'I think you are making a mistake, Hugh. If you really must do this you have to accept there is a chance you may never return here. If that happens, however, I will look after Baltasar and Andrea as though they were my own flesh and blood.'

'Thank you, Afonso.'

Hugh left his friend and returned to his house where his children were resting after crying themselves to sleep. Hugh was confident he would be home again in several months, and that they would then be able to rebuild their lives without his beloved Agnes. It briefly crossed his mind to give their daughter Agnes's cherished ring as she would no doubt one day marry, but decided against this as he didn't want to alarm her by thinking that he would not return.

Chapter 69

The Physicker

Father Ferraz stood next to the physicker in his building. The priest could not contain his frustration.

'I thought you were competent in such matters! We have already been paid. What are we to do?'

'Do not panic, Father. Although I am not well-versed in the art of embalming, I do know of a quick and easy method that will suffice.'

'Yes, and what is that?'

'We will submerge the woman in honey.'

'Have you gone mad? How will that preserve her?'

'As I say, Father, you need to trust me. I will arrange for a clay vessel to be built so we can place her inside and then fill it with honey. It can be used for the process of mummification – because of its extremely high sugar content it will act like salt.'

This was a less well-known use for honey; it would suck the water from bacteria, drying out any microbes so they could not survive.

'And how long will this take?'

'Send for the husband in three days' time. She will be ready for transportation once the clay vessel has been filled and placed inside a wooden crate. It will be heavy to carry. We can only pray that the clay does not crack on its journey.'

'Very well. I will return in three days' time. Do not let me down!'

The priest left for his church.

The physicker visited the local markets and acquired most of the stocks of honey that were for sale. These would be delivered by cart later that day, and he knew if he did not have enough he could always dilute it with salt water. He then arranged for an anthropoid ceramic coffin to be made. The local potter was given a description of what to make. He and the priest and would make a handsome profit, even after expenses. His final visit was to the local carpenter, whom he employed to make a sturdy wooden crate for the transportation of the coffin.

All his deliveries had arrived by the evening of the second day. The physicker had to employ three helpers due to the coffins weight. Agnes's body had been covered in blankets which had already been soaked in honey, so decomposition had been kept to a minimum.

The ceramic coffin had been made to the physicker's exact specifications. The physicker and his assistants then half-filled it with jugs of honey and gently placed Agnes's body inside, wrapped in the honey-soaked sheets. Once the honey level had settled, they continued to submerge her body using the remainder of the jugs, then placed the ceramic lid on top. The potter would return in the morning to seal the lid with fresh clay before the coffin was lifted into the wooden crate ready for collection.

The physicker paid the three helpers and was relieved to know that the next day the coffin would be gone.

Chapter 70

Left with a Friend

HUGH had felt guilty for not allowing their children to see Agnes's body, but he wanted to protect them and hoped they would remember her as a kind and caring mother. He felt as though his heart had been torn out after losing her, but busied himself with making arrangements with Afonso in the time before the priest's visit. Hugh had also ventured to the port in search of any ships that were bound for England. Most were sailing towards Africa, away from the conflict between England and France. Hugh had considered asking Captain Felstead, but he would not be returning for almost a month and Hugh was eager to travel now.

Eventually he found a ship that was travelling to northern Spain and was willing to sail to England for an exorbitant fee. The Portuguese trade cog was called the Amélia and she was carrying spices and wine to the Spanish sea port of Santander. The captain had agreed that, once she had been unloaded, he would sail north across the Bay of Biscay and keep to the west to avoid conflict. They would land on a far-western port on the Cornish coast. The fare Hugh had to pay would make the captain a rich man. He had heard about the tin mines in Cornwall, England. This unexpected journey there would enable him to purchase tin and resell it in the Algarve for further profit.

Afonso warned Hugh once again of the dangerous nature of the journey he was undertaking, but Hugh was determined to return the love of his life to her beloved homeland.

With all preparations now in place, the priest arrived at Hugh's home to notify him that Agnes was now ready for her journey to her final resting place. He gave Hugh directions on how to find the physicker in Tavira, then said his goodbyes and departed, no doubt to count how many coins he had earned.

Baltasar and Andrea knew their father was about to leave. Hugh put his arms around the two of them.

'It will not be long before I return, I promise. Come, now, you can take the horses and walk by our side to Afonso's house.'

The children were keen horse riders and felt proud to have been entrusted to look after their parents' horses. The short journey to Alfonso's house was a silent one, and the children walked slowly, knowing their father would be leaving once they had arrived. Afonso had always been kind to them and treated them like they were his own offspring, at least, which was one small consolation.

Once they arrived, Afonso came outside to greet them.

'Olá, Baltasar and Andrea. Go inside and help yourselves to some figs and almonds.'

'Sim, Afonso!'

They disappeared inside, where Afonso's wife and the rest of his family would spoil them with treats.

'It is a shame, Hugh, that my family are not as keen on the wine-making business as yours. I fear when you return yours will be bigger than mine!'

He was trying to be positive, but doubted that he would ever see Hugh again.

'Afonso, if I return, I will ask my children to bury me next to Agnes when I am gone. Perhaps if I die an old man, travel will be safer by then. Please take care of my children.'

Afonso was about to reply but Hugh had already started the short walk to Tavira. He had appreciated him sending the children inside, which had saved him saying a painful goodbye.

Chapter 71

The Amélia

HUGH found the physicker's home shortly after.

'Olá, senhor. Please come inside, your wife is ready for the journey ahead.'

'Obrigado.'

Hugh entered the dark building, which consisted of several rooms, and was led through to the one where the coffin awaited.

'All the preparations have been made for you, but there are two things which are essential for her transportation. The coffin itself is heavy and will require up to six men to lift onto a cart. It is important the crate does not become cracked, or the embalming properties inside may spill.'

Hugh had not been able to think clearly in his grief, and had therefore overlooked the fact that he would need help moving Agnes's body.

'Obrigado. I will return later with men to move my wife.'

Hugh then left to find the Amélia in the port where the captain agreed five of his crew would assist him in the transportation of Agnes's coffin. By late afternoon they had returned from the physicker's home after borrowing his horse and cart for the journey.

The loading of the Amélia was now almost complete; she was heavily laden with spices and almonds. The aroma from the sacks of food was wonderful. Hugh was aware the journey ahead would be expensive; despite Afonso's protests, Hugh had left half of his personal wealth with him in case he was not to return. The rest Hugh had hidden among the few possessions he was travelling with. He had learnt a harsh lesson from the pickpockets in London many years ago and did not want to make the same mistake again.

The Amélia left the port of Tavira on the high tide that evening. Hugh was apprehensive about returning to England, but his strong faith gave him the courage he needed. He too had missed Northumberland but was eager to return to his children once he had given Agnes a Christian burial. If all went to plan, he would be back in Tavira within a month or two.

Part Four
Homeward Bound

Chapter 72

At Sea Again

The Amélia started to journey westward along the Mediterranean coast; they passed the occasional fishing vessel and made good progress with a strong wind until they made a northerly turn. It would take them just under a week to reach the port of Santander.

The captain advised Hugh that it would be safer for him to remain on board once they arrived at the port. Although Hugh had resided in Portugal for many years, he still had a strong English accent which could have aroused suspicion, especially as France was only a short distance to the north.

The Amélia was unloaded and reloaded efficiently and was ready to sail north through the Bay of Biscay the following day. It would take just under six days to reach their destination on England's southwestern coast.

Luck was on Hugh's side: the weather was ideal, and a strong tail wind and experienced captain, an excellent navigator who had sailed to England twice before, helped them make quick progress.

Perhaps the most fortunate piece of luck on the journey was the fact that they spotted no other ships, friend or foe. With the commencement of Hundred Years' War, the ships' crews were more likely to be trigger happy with their cannons. Due to the relatively calm weather, the coffin remained undamaged.

Eventually, Hugh caught sight of the Cornish coast on the horizon. As most sea battles were taking place far to the east, in the English Channel, they would most likely be deemed a friendly ship on their approach to the coast. Many things had changed in England since Hugh had gone away; he had even missed the coronation of King Edward III.

The Amélia docked at Falmouth in the closing daylight hours. Fortunately, Hugh's English quickly quelled any suspicions the locals may have had and, in fact, when he relayed that the captain was keen to purchase tin, the crew was enthusiastically welcomed ashore.

Word soon got around. Hugh helped the captain to negotiate how much he could buy for the gold and silver coins that had been accepted throughout Europe since Roman times. Hugh waited patiently until the transaction had been concluded successfully.

He then enquired as to whether any locals would be willing to transport him and his coffin to London, and then on to Holy Island. No one had heard of such a destination, and when he asked how far it was to London the few who had made the journey said that it took at least ten days. Hugh replied that the total journey there and back would be over forty days. A roar of laughter went up among the group.

'Any person or persons willing to help me on such a journey will be handsomely rewarded; I will leave one hundred silver coins with your local priest as payment. Once we arrive, I will give you a phrase for you to repeat on your return so that your money can be released.'

The men who had gathered were murmuring among themselves – forty days away from home was a long time, but such a sum of money may be worth the effort.

Two men spoke out.

'We will help you, squire. Our two horses and cart can be ready for you to travel in the morning.'

'We have a deal.' Hugh replied. 'One hundred silver coins will be yours when you return.'

The two men were grinning, glad that they had spoken first.

'I will arrange your money and meet you at the ship in the morning, where the crew will help load my cargo onto your cart.'

'Yes, we will see you tomorrow.'

With that, Hugh left the small crowd to visit the local church, finding the priest inside.

'Father, I seek your help in the burial of my wife.'

Hugh went on to explain the agreement he had made with the two men who would transport Agnes. Money always talked, and when Hugh suggested he would make a donation to the church, the priest gladly accepted the task of holding the money.

'And what phrase have you chosen so I can make payment on their return?'

Hugh whispered it in his ear.

The night passed, and the two couriers arrived as the sun rose to midday as promised. The Amélia was currently being loaded with the remainder of the tin that the captain had purchased. He was eager to return to the Algarve with his bounty, and the fact that his ship was sitting dangerously low in the water did not concern him or his crew.

Hugh asked for the captain's assistance one final time, requesting that four of his crew help lift Agnes's coffin onto the carriage, where it was secured with ropes. The wooden load bed creaked slightly, but the oak construction was strong enough to bear the extra weight. However, the journey ahead would prove difficult for the horses.

Once the cart was loaded, Hugh said his farewells to the captain in Portuguese.

'Good luck, captain, and thank you for getting me here safely. Have a safe journey home.'

'Obrigado! I hope you manage to find a suitable burial place for your wife.'

The two men shook hands and the captain set sail almost immediately. No one would ever see the ship or its crew again, as the heavily laden vessel would find a watery grave in a storm two days later and all on board would be lost at sea.

Chapter 73

The Couriers

HUGH climbed on board the cart. The two couriers rode at the front and there was little conversation between them. In fact, they had not even introduced themselves to one another. Hugh preferred it that way and was glad to be riding next to Agnes. Again, good fortune played a part; although the track was narrow and steep in places, there had been little rain recently and it was dry and firm underfoot.

They headed steadily east, choosing to camp close to the track each night. Hugh sat by himself while the two men chatted to each other. On the fifth day, the track became much busier and wider as they approached London. So far, people had shown little interest in their travels. Hugh prayed each night that he would successfully complete his mission. He missed and worried about their children and hoped to return to them soon.

Now in unfamiliar territory, the two horsemen had to ask which road to take north from West London. Again, they attracted little interest as they headed north. Over a decade ago, Hugh and Agnes had travelled to London via a coal cog, so this area was unfamiliar to him too.

They were about five days into the journey north and the horses were struggling to pull the carriage. On Hugh's insistence and his money, they were replaced. Nevertheless, several days of rain had churned up the road with mud and, even with the new horses, they could not travel for two days until the ground became firm again. Hugh had also noticed a sticky substance seeping through onto the bed of the carriage, which was attracting wasps and other insects. He smelt the liquid and realised, to his surprise, that it was honey. Little did he know that the physicker had chosen a cheap, quick method to preserve his wife's body.

Over two weeks passed before they entered familiar territory. As they crossed the River Tyne, Hugh whispered to the coffin.

'Not long now, my darling. You are nearly home.'

Hugh gave the instruction to head east towards the coast once they had crossed the river. He knew it would be only be a few days before they approached Dunstanburgh Castle. He had contemplated burying Agnes in Embleton but had decided against it – even after the time he had been away, he could not risk being recognised. He was unware that Constable Binchester had been sentenced to death, thus reducing such a risk.

Suddenly, after twenty-three days of travel, the magnificent sight of Dunstanburgh Castle came into view. The castle had undergone a major upgrade in size since he was last here, and sea mist rolled intermittently over the beach in the murky light of the dawn. Hugh had mixed feelings about returning. The area was still as stunning as he remembered it with its golden beaches, rolling countryside and woodlands. But the suffering that Agnes had endured here made him angry.

A golden eagle flew above with a rabbit in its talons, still alive and struggling to get free. It landed on a nest in a nearby Scotch pine woodland, where its mate was waiting to feed their hungry, cawing eaglet.

Hugh had noticed there was another crack forming on the side of the coffin, causing more honey to seep onto the carriage bed. He was not overly concerned, however, as within a day or two he would arrive at Holy Island. That night, they all camped under the stars just outside the small village of Belford, which was at the forefront of the ongoing border conflict between the Scots and the English.

The sky was particularly clear and several shooting stars shot across the horizon.

Tomorrow Agnes would arrive at her final resting place.

Chapter 74

Familiar Territory

THE next day, all three travellers awoke just after dawn and headed north towards Beal after a breakfast of oats. By early afternoon they had arrived at the causeway over to Holy Island. The tide was starting to recede and, as they waited, all three men sat at the side of the cart, soaking up the sun. The two horsemen were in high spirits as they were close to their destination and a step closer to receiving their well-earned pay. When the tide was almost at its lowest point, they could see several horses starting to cross towards the mainland.

As the carriage entered the first part of the hard, wet sand on the causeway the wheels started to sink. They had only sunk a few inches, but this proved too much for the two horses to move, and they started to panic. One of the horsemen got down from the carriage to calm the horses; the other one had been inclined to whip them, but realised this would be futile as the carriage was completely stuck.

Hugh knew the coffin would have to be unloaded from the carriage.

'As you can see, the carriage will not move over the sand. I will go and fetch help. The coffin will need to be transported to the island by boat. Once the coffin has been loaded onto a boat you will be free to travel home.'

'Remember, we need the phrase to get our money!'

'Aye, I will give you that once my wife is safely on a boat.'

The two men looked at one another and nodded. There was no point in arguing; in any case, the coffin would have to be removed before they could travel home.

Hugh set off towards several small fishing boats that had been landed on the beach.

'Are there four men here who would like to earn money by helping me transport my wife's coffin over to the Holy Island?'

One of the fishermen looked at Hugh.

'Aye, if four of us were to help what would we get?'

'Ten silver coins each. Five now and five on arrival at St Mary's Church on the island.'

Four men stepped forward.

'Aye, we will help you.'

Hugh placed five silver coins in the palm of each man's outstretched hand. Although he had spent a lot of money, he easily had enough to pay for his return journey to the Algarve.

The men followed Hugh over to the stranded carriage on the causeway. The two horsemen looked relieved to see the fishermen arrive.

Hugh instructed them to unload the coffin from the carriage and place it on the beach. Once this was completed, the carriage moved easily. It made a small semi-circle turn and was back on firm land within minutes. Hugh walked up to the two horsemen.

'Here are ten more coins for your help. May God be with you on your return journey. When you see your priest, tell him the words, "Home, I remember forever."'

'We are sorry for the loss of your wife; she will be at peace in heaven now. We wish you a safe journey home and God bless you.'

They set off on their twenty-two-day journey home; they would arrive safely without incident and successfully claim their payment. They never forgot the man whose name they never knew who had shown such commitment to his wife.

Chapter 75

A Calm Sea

THE four fishermen helped Hugh to load Agnes's coffin onto the small fishing boat. It creaked under the strain. The boat was now ready for the tide to come back in, and at seven o'clock there was sufficient water for it to float. To reduce the weight, three of the fishermen had walked over to the beach outside St Mary's church on the island. Hugh said that he would help the other man row over to the island as he did not trust the task to anyone else and insisted he remain with the coffin at all times.

The two men started to row the distance of just over five miles to the church. Their journey was blessed with a final piece of luck. The sea was calm, like a mill pond, with only the slightest breeze behind them. The water was so clear that the sandy bottom could be seen. A shoal of mackerel swam underneath the boat and several large crabs could also be seen moving along the bottom. A loomery of puffins flew overhead towards the island; some had small fish in their mouths which they would feed on later.

There was plenty of daylight left on this summer's evening. Several large salmon could also be seen leaping, which created a large disturbance on the surface of the water.

After just over two hours of strenuous rowing, the small fishing boat landed on the beach outside St Mary's. Sweat covered the clothes on Hugh's back and blisters had formed on the palms on his hand. The fisherman who had rowed with him had hands which were strong as leather from all the years of hard work. Hugh drank greedily from a water jug handed to him by one of the others, who were waiting on the beach.

Once Agnes's coffin had been unloaded, he paid the men the remainder of the money he had promised them. They said their farewells, boarded the fishing boat and returned to the mainland in the fading light of the day.

Hugh sat on the beach next to the coffin and fell immediately fell into a deep sleep, content to know that Agnes would be buried the next day.

Hugh was woken early by a rustling sound. He sat upright quickly with his dagger in his right hand. A startled fox was licking the honey that was seeping from Agnes coffin. He waved his hand angrily and it scurried off into the undergrowth. There was a small population of foxes on the island which were often seen feeding on sea crustaceans at low tide.

Hugh went over to the coffin and cleaned off the fox hair that had stuck to the side. Although he was hungry, he ignored the rumblings in his stomach and went in search of the church priest. He found him moments later cooking a breakfast of mackerel with wild herbs. The priest looked up from his cooking fire and spoke to Hugh.

'Mornin'. I have plenty of food, would you like to join me? You look like you are hungry.'

'Aye, Father, that is kind of you. I will.'

'Here, sit down next to me; the food will be ready soon.'

'Thank you, Father.'

'Your accent sounds local – are you from here?'

'Aye, Father. I was born south of here but have been away for some time...'

Chapter 76

A Fallen Angel

THE priest often spoke to pilgrims to the island, which had become the base for Christian evangelism in the North of England, and was therefore used to sharing the bountiful resources of the sea with these people. He served up the meal and once they had finished Hugh spoke again.

'Father, on the beach behind us is the body of my wife who was once from these shores. We have travelled together from afar and I have returned her here to what I hope will be her final resting place, if you would be kind enough to help. She had a strong faith and this is where she would want to be.'

The priest was old, probably over sixty, which was an unusually high age to reach in this era. His beard was grey and he had a small smile on his kind face.

Hugh had pulled out a leather purse which he had noticed. He shook his head.

'I will help you. Put your money away.'

'Thank you, Father, you are too kind.'

This was one of the few people in his life including Thomas, Captain Felstead and Afonso who had offered genuine generosity and had not been influenced by the evils of money.

The priest could see that he was genuinely grieving and was glad to assist; he was a kind man and did not pry into the fate of this man's wife.

He walked with Hugh over to the edge of the graveyard, where Hugh made two further requests.

'Father, I wish to dig the grave myself, and ask that her grave remain unmarked.'

'Aye, as you wish. I will fetch you a shovel; come and find me when you have dug the grave.'

There were few gravestones in the churchyard. Hugh deliberately chose a plot near the southwestern corner where two walls joined. He made sure that there was no room for another grave between Agnes and the wall, as one day he himself intended to be buried there, allowing them to be together for eternity.

Once there was a suitable hole in the ground, Hugh went back to the coffin and smashed the ceramic with a spade. Honey poured out onto the beach and congealed in the sand. As Agnes had been wrapped in blankets, Hugh was spared the trauma of seeing her slightly decomposed body. The honey, with its miracle properties, had served its purpose. He then carried the sodden blanket concealing his wife's body and placed her gently into the fresh grave.

Hugh decided that Agnes's wedding ring should remain with her and placed it underneath the blanket, close to where her heart would be. The priest performed a brief Christian burial.

'Ashes to ashes, dust to dust, Amen.'

The priest then left Hugh at the graveside. He stood there for some time before he spoke softly.

'Someday, my darling, we will be together again. Until then, goodbye.'

He then returned to the beach and collected numerous pieces of the shattered ceramic coffin, gently placing them over her body before filling the rest in with soil. This would act as a barrier against any potential foxes, or even wolves, attempting to dig down. He had a few more tasks to attend to before setting off on his return journey to the Algarve.

By now it was mid-afternoon and the summer heat was quite intense. He returned to the beach and spent the rest of the day removing all evidence of the wooden crate and ceramic coffin. What would not burn he buried in the sand, and that night he made a large bonfire with the remaining wood.

The next morning, he purchased a beautiful journal, pheasant quill, and ink from a local merchant before commissioning a local stonemason to create a small headstone for Agnes's grave. The inscription read:

'Here rests a fallen angel. A.D. 1337.'

Chapter 77

The Journal

HUGH had noticed that building works had recently taken place in the church; this would make it easier for him to hide his journal once it was written. The stonemason had instructed him to return the next day for the small headstone he had ordered, so for the remainder of that day he frantically wrote in the journal using his new family surname. That evening, when it was complete, Hugh hid the journal behind a wooden panel in the newly constructed chancel.

The journal told of how he and Agnes escaped to the Algarve and mentioned Hugh's birth surname name, Parrock. This was to prove invaluable in tracing him. He also mentioned his brothers and military links. However, he did not elaborate on where in the Algarve they had settled, or the name of their vineyard, just in case the book was ever discovered. He also drew a map of the location of Agnes's grave and described the inscription on the headstone. The journal reiterated Hugh's belief of her innocence and how they adored both of their children.

His decision to leave the journal hidden rather than taking the book back to Algarve and instructing his children how to locate it upon his death may have been due to a premonition. Perhaps he felt the need to leave written evidence of Agnes's innocence in a house of God, or perhaps he needed reassurance that the journal would be safe, only to be discovered by those for whom it was intended.

The next day, Hugh collected the small headstone and proudly secured it above Agnes's grave. Everything was now in place and he made the decision to walk the journey of over fifty miles to the port of Newcastle, where he would take a coal cog to London like he did so many years ago and then a ship back to Portugal. Perhaps, by some chance, he would meet Captain Felstead again in London.

He said his farewells to the friendly, helpful priest. As he left, Hugh gave him his pheasant quill and ink as a parting gift. The quill was a fine specimen, with black strips spaced between the brown on the shaft.

'Thank you kindly, and have a safe journey back to whence you came, wherever that may be.'

'Aye, and thank you, Father, for your kindness and help.'

He then started his brisk walk to Newcastle, which would take him two full days.

Chapter 78

The Brothers

As Hugh approached the port of Newcastle, he noticed how much it had expanded in the years since he had been away. He was tempted to walk near his family home for old times' sake. Up until now he hadn't thought much about his brothers or father – were they even alive still? He certainly hadn't missed them, except for his mother, perhaps.

Hugh decided to avoid his family home and travelled directly to the docks, where he searched for a cog that was bound for London. He did not, however, take any notice of the approaching troops, which were under the command of Ranulphus Parrock, his eldest and cruellest brother. Ranulphus squinted in the closing light in the day and muttered to himself.

'Surely it can't be my urchin of a brother, Hugh? Perhaps he is here to challenge father's will?'

He spoke to his second in command.

'Take the men to the garrison; I have some urgent business to attend to!'

'Aye, sir!'

Ranulphus sidled over to a vantage point where he could not be seen by his younger brother. His father and younger brother, Edwyn, had been questioned many years before by the local sheriff about Hugh's desertion and role in enabling a convicted murderer to escape. They had been absolved of any blame, but the shame had taken its toll on their father's already poor health and he had passed away several years later. As Hugh had disappeared and was assumed dead, their father's estate had been split between two sons rather than three. Hugh's sudden reappearance could mean that this state of affairs was about to be challenged, unless of course Hugh was punished for his previous crimes...

Ranulphus watched Hugh board a coal cog and enter into a conversation with its captain. He was far too far away to be in earshot, but Ranulphus guessed that he was trying to negotiate passage on the vessel. He had to act quickly to make sure that Hugh could never return. He went to find the local sheriff, hoping all the while that Hugh would have left the city by the time he returned.

Hugh found a trade cog bound for London. He had a feeling of déjà vu, as he had made the same journey many years before. However, this time he was not being pursued and made no effort to disguise himself. In fact, his attire was that of a typical Portuguese middle-class man, so he stood out among the locals. Hugh was relaxed and the captain invited him aboard once he had paid his fare.

Fortunately, the ship was due to leave at high tide, within the hour.

Chapter 79

Wanted Dead or Alive

Ranulphus found a sheriff and spoke to him with authority.

'I need you and a group of men to escort me to the docks this instant. My younger brother, a common criminal, is about to escape. He must be arrested!'

The sheriff raised an eyebrow – people usually wanted to protect their own family – however he was duty bound to carry out this nobleman's instructions.

'Aye, sir, as you wish.'

He went inside and gathered six of his trusted men, who all grabbed their weapons. On their return Ranulphus commanded them to follow him.

The sheriff and his men duly followed Ranulphus the short distance to the cog. Initially, he could not see Hugh, but the back of his head came into view as the group approached.

Hugh was looking out to sea, thinking that he would soon be united with his children once again. He was unaware of the group of men about to board the ship.

The boarding party stormed onto the deck. The captain shouted out.

'By what authority do you come aboard?'

Ranulphus pushed him aside with his sword drawn.

'Get out of the way, man. You are harbouring a convicted criminal!'

The captain, realising he may lose the fare he was paid, took advantage of the commotion to hide the money between the planks of the deck. By now, the sheriff and his men had the cog surrounded.

Hugh spun his head around to see his elder brother confronting him with his sword. Hugh's heart was pounding at the shock of seeing him.

'You have brought shame on our family and are responsible for the death of our father. For that reason, you will be punished!'

Turning away from Hugh, he added,

'Over here, sheriff! Arrest this man!'

Hugh had suspected that his father would have passed away by now but was saddened all the same. Realising his brother had seen him and clearly wanted him arrested and tried for Agnes's escape, Hugh had to act quickly. He scanned the docks, noticing four guards, and then a further two, plus the sheriff who had already boarded. Hugh knew he could not fight his way out with his small dagger or try to outrun these men. There was only one other option. Without a word, he ran and jumped into the River Tyne. Hugh hit the surface of the cold, salty water and as he went underneath his dagger and the remainder of his money fell out of his clothing, down towards the bottom of the river. This did not concern him – all of his energy was focused on escaping and staying alive. Jumping into the river had been his best chance of escape, as it was unlikely that his pursuers could swim. However, although his elder brother was a proficient swimmer like him, Hugh knew he would be reluctant to spoil his extravagant clothing. If he did manage to escape and complete the arduous walk to London, he could consider waiting for Captain Felstead, although this could take months.

Hugh broke the surface of the water, catching his breath. He could see the south shore in front of him and started to swim frantically towards it, at odds with the strong current which moved him along at an angle. As a teenager he and his brothers would often swim in this river, a legacy of their late mother who had taught them how to swim at an early age. The distance of several hundred feet would be covered in a matter of minutes and he could then escape. It would take time to launch a rowing boat and the nearest bridge crossing was almost a mile away, giving Hugh a head start should they pursue. He would then run the distance of four miles or so to Marsden Grotto, a smugglers' cave where he could hide for several days in the hope that Ranulphus would give up his search. In his younger days, Hugh had enjoyed the tranquillity of the cave, especially if his brothers had been annoying him.

Ranulphus shouted at the sheriff.

'What are you waiting for, man? Jump in and get after him, he mustn't escape!'

'That is not possible, sir. We can't swim!'

Ranulphus had contemplated jumping in, but was more of a bully than a fighter and feared that, in his desperation to escape, his brother would cause him an injury.

'Well, order one of your men to shoot him before he gets out of range!'

'But sir, a moving target may be killed.'

'I don't care, you cretin! Just give the order, or I will inform your commanding officer. My brother is a criminal, wanted dead or alive.'

This threat was enough to force him into action. In any case, the sheriff reassured himself, at least three of his men and the captain could bear witness to the conversation if necessary.

He pointed at his best archer and gave the order.

'Fire at the prisoner at will!'

'Aye, sir!'

Chapter 80

The Archer

THE archer ran forward to the side of the cog and steadied himself. He then took an arrow from his leather shoulder bag, placed it in the wooden bow and took aim.

Some of the professional archers in this era were capable of firing up to four hundred yards, but Hugh was making steady progress towards the south shore and was almost out of an effective firing range. The cog was also bobbing slightly on the sea, making the shot even more difficult.

The archer closed his left eye and lined up the target with his right, pulling the bow back to its maximum tension. The wood creaked under the strain. There was a deadly silence on board, as no one wanted to disturb his intense concentration.

Moments later, he released the arrow. He had chosen a bodkin arrowhead that was both designed for a longer range and capable of penetrating light armour. For this particular shot, though, it wasn't an issue as Hugh was only wearing light clothing.

Hugh had seen a suitable landing point on the bank ahead, but not once did he turn around to see if he was being pursued. This would cost him precious time. He was over halfway and had covered nearly one hundred and thirty yards when he felt an excruciating pain in his left shoulder, accompanied by cheering in the distance. He stopped, standing upright in the water, and placed his right hand over the shaft of the arrow on his left shoulder. He judged from the point of entry that the arrow had almost gone completely through. With his training he had been told to be careful in removing arrows as the barb was designed to stay in the flesh and, if withdrawn, would tear further tissue.

As the arrow had almost gone through his body, the only way was forward. Hugh placed his shirt in his mouth and gripped down hard with his teeth. Then, with all his strength, he pushed the arrow further into his body. The agony almost caused him to pass out. Slowly, the arrow moved forward and, within seconds, the tip of the arrow pierced the skin near his left armpit. Once he could see the wooden shaft clear of his skin, he snapped the arrow just below the arrow feathers. He did not want to drag these through his body as they would cause an infection should they come off inside him. He then moved his right hand to the front of his body and pulled the remainder of the arrow clear. The water around him turned crimson red with blood; he removed his shirt from between his teeth and started to pant. The pain was agonising.

The men aboard the cog cheered as the first shot of the arrow hit Hugh and he stopped swimming instantly. Ranulphus pointed at the archer.

'Well done, my man! A gold coin will be paid to thee for such a fine shot!'

'Thank you, sir!'

He then turned to the sheriff.

'My dear fellow, you are to commandeer a rowing boat and capture that man!'

'Aye, sir!'

The sheriff sprang into action as this nobleman had already promised a gold coin to the archer. Surely he would be rewarded for the fugitive's capture? Enthusiastically, he and his men quickly acquired a rowing boat and started to row towards where Hugh was treading water.

Adrenalin had kicked in and the pain in Hugh's body had subsided ever so slightly. He rolled onto his back and, using his legs only, continued to swim towards the south shore.

The rowing boat had now passed the cog and would soon reach Hugh. The smile on Ranulphus's face faded as he realised Hugh was moving once again. He looked at the archer, who had remained on board, and shouted at him,

'What are you waiting for, man? Take aim again at once!'

'Sir, the rowing boat is in my line of fire.'

'I don't give a damn. Shoot or I will have you punished!'

Not wanting to disobey, the archer decided to take a shot, but he knew he could not be punished for missing at such a long range. The rowers were closing the gap and he didn't want to accidentally shoot one of his men. He knelt down and lined up a shot which was wide and safe to the left. He delayed as long as he dared before releasing the arrow. All the time, the rowing boat was closing the gap. The arrow launched and landed harmlessly in the sea over twenty feet to left of Hugh's head.

'You moron, you have missed! Take aim again!'

But as he said this an arm grabbed Hugh's leg in the water.

'No need, sir, the prisoner has been caught.'

Ranulphus pushed by the archer and walked to the side of the docks, exclaiming,

'I can see that, you cretin!'

Perhaps, the archer thought, when the commander had calmed down, he would receive his gold coin.

Chapter 81

An Old Friend

HUGH could hear and see a rowing boat approaching. Clearly, their intention now was to capture and not to kill. With a serious injury, no weapon and no money to bribe, the odds were stacked against him. Several minutes later, he felt a pair of hands roughly grab his feet. Hugh kicked out to free himself but this made no difference as another guard grabbed him. He was unceremoniously shoved to the back of the rowing boat, where his hands and feet were shackled by one of the men.

'Hold on to the prisoner,' the sheriff called to his men. 'He may try to jump overboard!'

Hugh sat, shackled and soaking wet, in the boat. His shoulder was now throbbing with pain, but none of this came close to the grief he felt in losing Agnes. He thought of their children back in the Algarve and prayed they were coping well with Afonso. It now seemed unlikely that they would ever be reunited.

When the rowing boat arrived back at the dock, Hugh was dragged onto the pier where Ranulphus was waiting. Seeing his younger brother standing in front of him, he slapped him deliberately on his injured shoulder.

'You are a common criminal and I am ashamed to call you my brother!'

The pain in Hugh's shoulder was so intense he passed out. When he awoke, several hours later, he was in a darkened cell. Blood had congealed in his wound and the pain had not subsided. His hand shackles were attached to the wall and he was alone in the cell. Here he sat for several days, with minimal food and water, until his fate was decided.

Ranulphus had decided to head north to discuss his captured brother with John de Lilburn, Constable of Dunstanburgh Castle. When John heard the news he replied,

'If you have come here to plea for your brother's life, you are wasting your time. Constable Binchester was sentenced to death by drowning for his incompetence for allowing a convicted murderer to escape. In his absence, your brother was also sentenced to death for aiding her escape. He was due to be hung, drawn and quartered and this punishment still stands now that he has been captured. The law must be upheld!'

Ranulphus responded with a slight smile.

'And I will ensure this is carried out.'

He already knew what punishment had been issued to Hugh and had travelled only here to ensure the execution was still valid. He felt a small pang of guilt as Hugh's method of execution was particularly barbaric. He said his goodbyes and then returned to Newcastle Gaol with the freshly issued execution warrant with which he had been entrusted. He knew that John de Lilburn would soon check to see if it had been carried out. He would now inform his younger brother, Edwyn, that Hugh had been captured and was due to be executed in two days' time. He was secretly pleased that Hugh was alive but reality quickly set in regarding his imminent execution.

After Ranulphus had left, Edwyn went to find Hugh's friend Thomas who was stationed at the local garrison, assuming he wasn't on manoeuvres. Over the years Thomas had steadily worked his way up through the ranks.

Edwyn arrived at the garrison and enquired as to Thomas's whereabouts. Thomas was shocked to hear Edwyn's news of Hugh.

'I never knew what happened to Hugh and I am glad he and Agnes escaped – but why come back now and jeopardise his freedom?'

'That is a mystery. Hopefully we will have the opportunity to ask him. If we go to the gaol now, I will bribe the guards to let us see him. It may prove difficult, however, as Ranulphus has increased the number of guards in case he tries to escape.'

They left the garrison and made the short walk to the gaol. Edwyn successfully managed to bribe the guards and they were allowed to visit Hugh for a short time. The first thing they noticed was the putrid aroma. Hugh's wound was infected and oozing puss, his flesh pale and his eyes dull. Thomas spoke first.

'Greetings, my dear friend, it has been a long time.'

'Aye, it has. Good to see you and my brother. I'm sorry for all the upset I have caused.'

'Somehow we will help you escape!'

Edwyn was shocked to hear this – Thomas had not discussed it with him. He would help, as he did not hate Hugh like their eldest brother; Edwyn also suspected that Ranulphus thought Hugh had returned for money.

'Dear brother, why return now?'

Hugh decided he could not trust anyone and would not reveal that he was a father, where he had lived and the fact he had buried Agnes to the north, so he lied.

'Agnes never made it. She drowned during our escape. I have lived in London all this time and I foolishly returned now to try and prove my innocence.'

There was an awkward silence, which Hugh broke with a wry laugh.

'But I failed.'

There was a loud bang on the door and the guard entered the cell.

'Time to leave!'

As Thomas stood up he whispered to Hugh.

'I will come back tomorrow.'

They left the cell. Once they were out of earshot, Edwyn turned to Thomas in concern.

'Thomas, you do realise it will be impossible for us to help Hugh escape?'

'Aye, I said it to raise his spirits but he knew we couldn't. Besides, even if we could, you no doubt saw his infected wound… He wouldn't make it.'

Edwyn contemplated this.

'But he will receive an excruciating death.'

'Edwyn, if you trust me, I will take care of things.'

'I can't see how you can but, yes, I trust you. I don't want Hugh to suffer. I think even Ranulphus has regrets because of the punishment issued. He must have thought a simple hanging would have sufficed.'

Edwyn left without another word. Thomas walked with purpose in the opposite direction. He knew what he had to do.

Chapter 82

No Hope

THE next day, Thomas returned to the gaol and successfully secured a brief visit with Hugh. There was a different guard on duty and he insisted he stayed in the cell during the visit.

It pained him to see his best friend suffer. His condition had deteriorated since the previous day and his eyes were bright with fever.

'Hello, Thomas, good to see you again.'

Hugh looked into his eyes. Although Thomas was a trusted friend, there would be no point in telling him the truth about Agnes's burial. In any case, there was now no hope of him being buried next to her, as he had wished. He contemplated asking Thomas to travel to the Algarve to inform his children he would not ever be coming home, but with the outbreak of war it was a risk only he himself would have been prepared to take.

'You are a kind man, a good friend, and I thank you for all your help.'

The guard was becoming impatient.

'Time to go. If his brother catches us here we will both be for it.'

Thomas gripped Hugh's hand and discreetly placed a pellet in his palm.

'Goodbye, dear friend. I hope you find strength from within.'

Hugh nodded as Thomas left the cell, followed by the guard. The door was slammed shut and then locked. He waited a few minutes and then opened his palm. It contained a moist food-like pellet. Hugh guessed that it was a poison – Thomas must be offering him an alternative from the execution he was due to receive tomorrow.

To be hung, drawn and quartered was a truly awful way to die. The condemned person was first fastened to a hurdle or wooden panel, and then drawn by horse to the place of execution, where they were hanged to the point of death. They were then emasculated, disembowelled, beheaded and chopped into four pieces. Their remains were often displayed in prominent places such as bridges and such a punishment was usually reserved for high treason. Women found guilty of this were usually burned at the stake.

It had been deemed unlikely that Hugh would ever return, so such a severe sentence had been intended to serve primarily as a deterrent to others.

Chapter 83

Edwyn's Suggestion

HUGH looked at the pellet, contemplating his choices. His shoulder wound was infected and was unlikely ever to heal, even if he could escape, and his execution would be unimaginably painful. Tears started to form in his eyes as he resigned himself to the fact he would not ever see Baltasar and Andrea again. Neither would he ever know that, although the two of them grieved for both of their parents, they both flourished in Tavira. As promised, Afonso, continued to care for them as though they were his own children and in 1386, under the Treaty of Windsor, his future grandson would benefit from improved trade links. The family wine business would provide huge financial success in the future. However, the family association with Northumberland would be lost for centuries to come.

Thomas had made a cruel but kind decision in giving him the poison pellet. The previous day, Thomas had gone in search of a local medicine man that could provide an alternative for Hugh. He purchased a simple concoction, of which the primary ingredient was *digitalis purpurea*. Even small amounts of foxglove could be fatal.

Hugh placed the pellet in his mouth and swallowed it whole. He lay down on his right side and relived in his mind all the good times he and Agnes had shared. He was now at peace with the world. Hugh passed away shortly afterwards from a massive heart attack.

The guard entered the cell with Hugh's evening meal several hours later, only to find his dead body. The guard promptly went to inform his superiors of his discovery. Ranulphus and Edwyn were duly informed of their brother's death. Edwyn correctly guessed that Thomas had somehow saved him from his impending execution and Ranulphus was glad Hugh was dead, although secretly pleased that he wouldn't have to witness the execution. Thomas and Edwyn would not meet again during the remainder of their lives.

Edwyn broached the subject of Hugh's funeral.

'My dear brother, whatever Hugh has done in his life I feel that it is only right that he should be buried in the family tomb at St Andrew's Church.'

'Nonsense.' Ranulphus replied. 'I will have his body thrown into the Tyne with the rest of the sewage!'

Their father, Sir Robson Parrock, had been knighted shortly before his death and, as a man of distinction, was granted a tomb inside the church. Their mother, who had passed away many years earlier, was buried in the churchyard. Robson's will and testament had specified he was to be buried with his three sons. It had not been altered when Hugh had disowned the family. Ranulphus and Edwyn argued for most of the day until they finally came to a compromise.

'What if Hugh was to be buried inside his own coffin next to our father's? That way, we are almost together, but still separate.'

Ranulphus's temper had receded and he was growing tired of the argument. Perhaps Edwyn's suggestion wasn't such a bad one after all. A tomb that would eventually contain a father and two sons, with a separate one next to it, would be a clear display to the world that there was a rift in the family.

Edwyn had viewed this differently. Personally, he considered that that all the family would be together in the same churchyard, and therefore not separated.

'If I agree to this, Edwyn, will you never mention Hugh's name again for as long as you live?'

'Aye, brother, it is settled, thank you. I will make all the arrangements.'

And this was the outcome; the Parrock family were buried in and around St Andrew's Church and Hugh's name was never mentioned again.

At least Hugh and Agnes were buried in the same county, if not together.

Part Five

Holy Island, 1963

Chapter 84

Tavira 369288

Reverend Collins called the Archbishop the next morning to relay the discovery Marjorie had made in the wine shop. He was surprised and told the reverend that he would investigate further.

That Sunday, Reverend Collins served one of the bottles of wine at communion. The phone call came the following day.

'Reverend Collins, glad I could catch you in. It appears your search is indeed over – the name is an exact match. The reason why it was initially overlooked is that it was always assumed that the family name had been reversed as a deliberate marketing ploy. To indicate that their wines were unique, I suppose. Apparently, the business is one of the wealthiest wine producers on the Algarve and is the only known name in the country with that combination! Because you were the one who made the discovery, I will let you have the honour of contacting the current heirs directly. I am still waiting for their home telephone number, but I will post this information to you when possible.'

'I appreciate you letting me make the call, Archbishop. It will be a real honour.'

'I will put all the information you need in the letter. I require written permission from the Diocese of Hexham and Newcastle to have the Holy Island body exhumed, verified and then reburied in the same grave. Once it is confirmed, we can arrange a suitable date for all those concerned. I will be in touch.'

'Of course, Archbishop, and thank you once again.'

He replaced the receiver and went to find his wife to tell her the good news. As a celebration, he poured them both a large sherry.

The following week, a large enveloped arrived at the Rectory containing all the information as promised. He called his wife to him and, ensconced in his study, nervously prised open the envelope with a silver letter opener.

He briefly read the contents and found the page that contained the direct phone number of the Serafim-Santos family. He exchanged an apprehensive glance with his wife.

'Well, dear, as there is no time difference I suppose I'll give them a call.'

'Good luck! I'll leave you to make the call in private.'

Before he could ask her to stay, she had already left his study and closed the door. He sat there for a few minutes, gathering his composure, and then dialled the operator.

'Operator, how may I help?'

'Er, yes. Can you connect me to Tavira, Portugal 369 288, please?'

'One moment please, sir, while I try to connect you.'

There was a pause and then static could be heard over the line as the operator was making the connection.

A female voice answered the phone.

'Residência de Olá Serafim-Santos.'

'Hello, do you speak English?'

'Um momento por favor, vou buscar o senhor Serafim-Santos.'

The reverend guessed that she was going to fetch someone that spoke English, so he held on the line. He was conscious of the cost of being connected to Portugal but did not hang up. A few minutes later a man with a European accent spoke in impeccable English.

'Good morning, this is Senhor Serafim-Santos, how may I be of assistance?'

'Good morning. My name is Reverend Collins and I am calling from Holy Island in Northumberland, England. I have made a discovery which concerns your family. It dates back over six hundred years.'

The rather sceptical man on the other end of the line replied,

'I see, and how much will this discovery cost me?'

'My apologies for not explaining better. I am not asking for money. Quite the opposite, in fact. Our local church was damaged in a storm earlier this year and a book was discovered dating back to the late fourteenth century which mentions your family name. I can only assume it regards your forefathers. We would like to invite you and your family here, to the island, to attend a special burial service.'

The man, who was still rather sceptical, replied,

'I see. If you have a pen and piece of paper handy I will give you the contact details of my secretary here at Tavira. If you could send her the information I would appreciate that.'

'Yes, of course, that would be splendid. If I could have the contact details, please.'

The details were passed to the reverend, after which Senhor Serafim-Santos replaced the receiver and returned to his wife, who was sunbathing by the pool in their magnificent villa overlooking the sea.

'Who was that on the phone, darling?'

'Oh, some crazy English man claiming to have something belonging to my family from six hundred years ago!'

'It's a good thing we took the day off today, then!'

Carlos Serafim-Santos was the current owner of Serafim-Santos wines and, as a multi-millionaire, could afford to employ trusted people to run his successful business. He had assumed his family all originated from the Algarve. He had given the correct address for his company just in case the English man was telling the truth. He was an astute business man and had received his fair share of crank calls over the years. There had been something sincere in the English man's voice, but only time would tell.

Chapter 85

A Distant Relative

TEN days later, a letter arrived address to the Secretary of Serafim-Santos wines. Carlos had instructed her that, if such a letter arrived, she was to bring it to him immediately. Once she had opened it, she passed the letter to her boss in his plush office overlooking his large vineyard. He placed the letter, which was formal and embossed by the Diocese of Hexham and Newcastle, on his desk. The letter explained much of what had taken place on the telephone conversation and there was indeed an invitation for him and his family to attend a special burial ceremony on Holy Island, England, in four weeks' time.

Carlos was now convinced it was a genuine invitation and, as there no mention of any money he had to pay, he asked his secretary to arrange a flight to London one week prior to the event. He and his wife, Ana, were overdue a holiday and neither had travelled to England before. Carlos had only recently married and they had no children yet. He was an only child and his parents had passed the family business to him several years ago as they were now enjoying their retirement. He rang them to see if they would like to join both Ana and him on this adventure. They declined, suspecting it was hoax, but wished their son a safe trip.

When he returned home that night, Ana was excited to be going to England. She had read in glossy magazines about the luxury shops that were in the Knightsbridge area of London. Shopping was one of her favourite pastimes. She herself was from a wealthy family that had made its fortune in fashion.

Due to their business interests, they were both fluent in English, so language would not be a problem for them. Carlos arranged their travel visas and they were soon booked on a Starways flight to London, first class.

Over the next week, Carlos gave his deputy instructions for when he was away. His father said that he would also drop in from time to time to check on the business.

The day before they were due to travel, Carlos picked up his new red sports car for which he had been waiting for some time. He would have to reluctantly leave this at the airport until he returned.

Chapter 86

The Flight

'Come along now, darling! We are going to be late for the flight!'

'Yes, yes, I am coming!'

Usually, Carlos had to round up his wife when they were about to go out, but as she was excited it was her who was eager to leave.

They left their villa and drove the twenty miles to Faro airport in a new Ferrari 250 gto. They arrived in plenty of time thanks to Carlos's high-speed driving. The four-litre v12 created a phenomenal amount of power; no other car could even attempt to keep up with him on the road.

Once at the airport, the valet looked eagerly at the gleaming red sports car. Carlos handed him the keys along with a rather generous one-thousand-escudo note.

'Don't even think about it', he said, wryly. 'She has just under one hundred kilometres on the clock and I expect the same when I return.'

'Sim, senhor!'

Carlos and Ana waited in the first-class lounge of Starways Airlines, and were aboard the Douglas C-47B Dakota, sipping champagne, within thirty minutes. The plane would take just over four hours to complete its journey to Heathrow.

'I have made reservations for us at the Ritz hotel. Fortunately, the reverend in England gave me a list of contacts in the north, so when we land I can book the accommodation there. We should have several days sightseeing and shopping before our train leaves.'

'How wonderful, I particularly look forward to the shopping part!'

Carlos knew this part of the trip would be costly, but it was worth it to see his new wife happy.

He was reading an onboard magazine which contained an article about the infamous Flying Scotsman train that was scheduled to be decommissioned later that year and replaced by a more modern diesel engine. He decided they would travel first class on this magnificent-looking train. The article concluded by stating that the Flying Scotsman has been described as the world's most famous steam locomotive.

They both drifted off to sleep before the plane was an hour into its journey. The next thing they knew was the stewardess waking them for the descent into Heathrow.

Chapter 87

The Flying Scotsman

THEIR plane arrived on time and, when the Dakota had switched off its engines, all the passengers disembarked and entered the terminal building. As first-class passengers, Carlos and Ana were fast tracked through immigration control. As she walked down the corridor dressed in a modern miniskirt which showed off her long dark legs, Ana caught the attention of the male members of staff.

'Blimey, Jeff, you see the pins on that bird?'

'She's out of your league, mate! She's a port out and starboard home!'

Another man wolf whistled, hoping to catch her attention. Carlos smiled at his wife, whose beauty was admired wherever they travelled. They had now collected their baggage and moved to the outside taxi rank, where they spoke to the first available driver.

'Where to, guv?'

'The Ritz, please.'

''Ere, sir, let me help you with your luggage.'

The driver was always helpful to his customers and, with a destination like the Ritz, was hoping for a large tip.

The first thing Carlos and Ana noticed about London was how much cooler the weather was. They enjoyed the sights on the journey to the Ritz with an enthusiastic commentary from the taxi driver. Once they had entered the city of London itself the traffic levels had increased slightly. As this was the 1960s, major congestion was a thing of the future.

As they drove through Piccadilly Circus, a large billboard advertising the forthcoming James Bond movie, *From Russia with Love*, sparkled above them. The iconic red London buses, adverts for Typhoo tea, Oxo and Meccano plastered on their sides, filled the roads.

On arrival at the Ritz the cabbie swiftly attended to his passengers, not wanting to miss out on his tip. He was not disappointed, as Carlos handed him several ten-shilling notes.

'Cheers, gov!'

The cabbie drove off in high spirits. He could now afford to watch his favourite football team play at Stamford Bridge.

The concierge greeted Carlos and Ana as though they were long-lost friends.

'Welcome to the Ritz, sir and madam. If there is anything you require please do not hesitate to ask.'

This iconic five-star hotel was known throughout the world for its opulence and exceptional level of service. Carlos already regretted only booking a three-night stay.

Over the forthcoming days, Ana managed to put a serious dent in Carlos's holiday money fund. As promised, the concierge had managed to secure them two first-class tickets for the following morning on the ten o'clock King's Cross to Edinburgh Flying Scotsman service.

On the morning of their departure, the hotel had arranged a chauffeur to take them to the train station. The almost-new Rolls Royce Silver Cloud III arrived after their breakfast to transport them to the station, where there was a flurry of activity. They passed street traders, including people selling newspapers and freshly cooked chestnuts. Porters were busy assisting the passengers to their cabins. The magnificent green coloured steam locomotive, which had covered almost two million miles during its service, had officially reached a speed of one hundred miles an hour three decades before.

The LNER Class A3 4472 engine was fired up and ready to go. At exactly ten o'clock, a whistle was blown and the train departed the station. Within minutes she was approaching cruising speed. There would be a few stops on the way for passengers and for the tender to refill with water and coal.

Carlos and Ana would disembark in Alnwick Station in Northumberland, which would not close for almost another five years.

The Flying Scotsman was punctual. Once outside the station they waited at the taxi rank and asked to be taken to the nearest car rental firm. The short journey took less than five minutes. Jim's Autos had various cars available to rent including a Mini, Morris Minor and a Ford Anglia. None of these particularly excited Hugh. Towards the back of the forecourt was an almost new 1963 Jaguar E-Type Series 1 in British racing green. Having spotted the car, Carlos announced,

'That's the car I wish to hire!'

'Sorry, sir, that's not for rent.'

'Name your price!'

The Jaguar was the garage owner's pride and joy and he had worked and saved hard to purchase this prestigious marque. He had also had a little help from 'Ernie' the computer, which generated premium bond winners. The thousand-pound win had paid for almost half the car.

Jim hesitated, not knowing how much to ask. Was ten pounds a day too much to ask, he thought?

'I will pay one hundred of your English pounds for a week!'

Jim thought he had won on the bonds again.

Carlos peeled off the cash from the wad in his wallet and gave it to Jim.

'Please enter the office, sir, and we will fill out the paperwork.'

Once this was completed, Jim reluctantly handed over the keys for the Jaguar. Carlos turned over the ignition and the engine roared to life, purring as it sat on tick over.

'Could you give me directions to the Holy Island, please?'

'Aye, I will fetch you a map.'

Jim returned with an Esso Road Map of Northern England. As he talked Carlos through the route, he added,

'And sir, please, pay attention to the tidal crossings. This is a valuable car!'

Many a driver had appeared to heed such warnings before having their vehicles flooded and written off. Fortunately, Reverend Collins had sent Carlos a safe crossing timetable for their imminent meeting.

'Relax; if I return her with one scratch I will buy you a new one!'

Jim did not doubt this for a minute. Carlos revved the car and pulled out onto the B6346, heading towards the A1 at high speed.

Ana switched on the car radio and they both laughed and sang along to a song after her namesake by the Beatles.

Carlos was enjoying driving the car and, once on the A1, he accelerated hard and the car responded.

'Darling, the speed here is miles, not kilometres an hour!' Ana joked.

They almost missed the turn for Holy Island due to the speed of his driving. They arrived at the causeway and, as expected, the tide was out. They were thirty minutes early as they parked on the drive of the Rectory.

Chapter 88

Handing Over the Journal

REVEREND Collins, his wife, Marjorie, and Rufus all came outside to greet their guests.

'Mr Serafim-Santos, I presume?'

'Yes. Reverend Collins, I presume?'

The men shook hands and all the introductions were made, including Rufus.

'My wife has kindly prepared an afternoon tea for us in the garden. We can discuss the proceedings of the next few days there.'

Once they were all seated and the tea was served, Reverend Collins started to discuss the purpose of Carlos and Anas' visit.

'I hope you have had a pleasant stay in England so far. I understand it is your first visit here?'

'Yes, it is. My wife and I also enjoyed a brief stay in London after we landed; in fact, after our train journey north we came straight here and will check into our hotel later. We will be staying at the Dunstanburgh Castle Hotel in Embleton and hope to explore the area before the service in two days' time.'

'I see. You have chosen a beautiful area to visit and no doubt wish to see Dunstanburgh Castle, where Agnes once lived. Regarding the service and the history of your family, it is a mystery to our local historians why it was never retrieved by Hugh's children. We can only guess that for whatever reason he sadly never made it back to the Algarve and it would therefore be conjecture to suggest reasons why. The journal gives us clear evidence that there should be pieces of ceramic used to shield Agnes's body from vermin. At the service we will be able to hopefully witness the discovery of this. In the journal there is a mention of a headstone. Sadly, as over six hundred years have passed, the headstone face above the grave has been weathered away. At least, with verification, we will be able to confirm the resting place of your distant grandmother. I must say, after the discovery of the journal we made every effort to trace you and it is thanks to Marjorie that you are here today.'

Reverend Collins then picked up a small package that was wrapped in brown paper with thin white string holding it together.

'Mr Serafim-Santos, it is my great pleasure to present to you your distant grandfather's journal.'

'Thank you, that is most kind. I will treasure it and ensure it is passed down to future generations.'

Ana smiled at her husband's comment, as they had been enthusiastically trying for their first child since the day they had married.

'I would also like to add, as there is clear written evidence in the journal of Hugh's belief that Agnes was innocent, I have been advised that you may be able to pursue a legal challenge and clear her name. I have also been advised that this case would be unique and there would have been little or no defence for Agnes back then, so it is worth a try.'

'You are most kind. I will get my lawyers to look into this on my return to the Algarve. My wife and I have also bought a gift for you; please excuse me while I fetch it.'

Carlos left the table and collected from the boot of the Jaguar a wooden case containing three bottles of wine.

'I have written to the Archbishop of Newcastle with a suitable donation to the church to cover all your expenses, and I wish to present to you a bottle each of our 1897 vintage wine. It was an exceptional year.'

In fact, his donation to the church was five thousand guineas, which was a phenomenally generous amount, and each bottle of wine was valued at one hundred pounds, also a large amount of in the 1960s.

As Carlos handed Marjorie her bottle, the reverend said, jovially,

'Try not to drop that one!'

They laughed and explained to Carlos how she had discovered the family name.

'Senhora', Carlos replied, 'if you knew this bottle's value you probably would drop it in shock!'

This time, everyone at the table laughed, although Marjorie's was slightly nervous.

They continued talking into the afternoon. Thirty minutes before the tide was due to come back in, Carlos announced,

'As the tide is approaching, it is time for my wife and I to depart. Thank you for your hospitality and for returning my grandfather's journal to me. We will explore the island on the day of the service as time is now against us, and we look forward to seeing you again then.'

'Aye, it's my pleasure. We'll look forward to seeing you both again in two days' time.'

Carlos and Ana drove across the causeway just as the tide was starting to come in and headed towards Embleton.

Chapter 89

Castle Ruins

Carlos and Ana checked into the Dunstanburgh Castle Hotel. Through reception, he booked a round of golf at the local golf club for the next afternoon, along with an evening salmon fishing on the River Aln. Ana said she was tired after all the travelling and would explore the local area while Carlos pursued these sports. The highlight of the next morning, however, would be a short walk to Dunstanburgh Castle.

That evening, they had a delightful meal in the hotel made from locally produced food. They both had a crab pâté starter followed by a lamb shank, for which the meat had been locally sourced. Carlos and Ana both sampled some of the local mead.

They then returned to their room for a night of passion. In the morning they consumed a large plate of Craster kippers for breakfast. They were given directions of how to get to the castle; the weather was glorious with only the slightest breeze. As they walked down Sea Lane to the coast, Carlos noticed a house for sale in The Villas. He made a mental note of the estate agent's name on the sale board; he would speak to them on their return to Algarve and purchase the house as a surprise for Ana. They had both fallen in love with the county and he intended to return here for numerous holidays. The house for sale was perfect as it had views of the castle. As they approached the castle from the beach, Carlos eagerly looked at the golf course on which he would soon be playing.

They then walked past Greymare Rock. He commented on its bizarre formation and, for no apparent reason, he felt the hairs lift on his neck. They paused here and were both in complete awe of the castle, which was now in a state of ruin. Carlos was busily taking photos on his Leica M3 camera. They spent several hours exploring the castle. Hugh had made a brief mention in his journal that Agnes had once lived here.

Afterwards they walked the short distance to Craster and enjoyed a light lunch of fresh crab salad in the local pub. Ana drank slim line tonic water and Carlos sampled some of the local ale. After lunch they walked hand in hand on the beach, collecting small pieces of green glass which had been smoothed by numerous tides over the years. Carlos had plans to have some of them made in to jewellery for Ana.

They returned to the hotel for an afternoon siesta and, until the day of the service, spent their time either resting playing golf, salmon fishing on the River Aln or exploring Alnwick and the local area.

Chapter 90

The Service

Carlos and Ana drove to Holy Island early on the day of the service. They would be taking the late service of the Flying Scotsman back to London that day. They managed to explore the island, including the priory, before a light drizzle began to fall. Shortly before the allotted time of the service, Carlos and Ana met at the church and the introductions were made. Even the local press had sent a small number of representatives; there was much public interest in a burial service spanning over six hundred years.

At exactly midday the Archbishop started the proceedings by announcing that the site of Agnes's grave would be investigated to determine if there was any ceramic object in it.

They all stood next to the suspected location of Agnes's grave and the two gravediggers started to turn the soil. All eyes were hoping to see fragments of her clay coffin being discovered. Ten minutes of strenuous digging had passed and nothing of significance had been found then, all of a sudden, there was a change in the tone of the shovels as they entered the ground.

'I think I've discovered what you're looking for!' one of the gravediggers shouted.

The excited group huddled closer as one of the diggers picked up a piece of ceramic from the ground and passed it to Reverend Collins.

'Well, ladies and gentlemen, it looks as though we've discovered the grave of Agnes Serafim-Santos, née Weaver. We will now be able to erect a headstone with her name. A shame, of course, that we never discovered her husband.'

Just as he said this, a black Ford Thames 400E van arrived and parked in front of the gates. Two pall bearers got out and nodded towards the grinning Archbishop.

'I would like to announce the arrival of Hugh Parrock, also known as Hugh Serafim-Santos!'

Reverend Collins was astounded and a gasp rang out among the group

'But how is this possible?'

'My apologies for not revealing this sooner, but I only got confirmation after Mr and Mrs Serafim-Santos had left the Algarve so I decided to reveal the surprise today. Let me explain. It was a major piece of luck, really. I was discussing the journal at a recent meeting when the organist at St Andrew's church in Newcastle announced there were two graves inside which bore the Parrock family name. I then visited the church and, lo and behold, there they were. As they were inside the building, their inscriptions had been protected from the elements. All the names match those in Hugh's journal and the era is correct. I had an additional exhumation order made and here we are today. Today we will be able to carry out Hugh Serafim-Santos's wishes, as per the instructions in the journal he once wrote.'

The small wooden box containing the remains of Hugh was then passed to Carlos.

'I think it would be fitting if you were to lay him to rest in Agnes's grave so that your ancestral bloodline can now be reunited for eternity after all these years apart.'

Carlos knelt down by the graveside and gently placed the wooden box in the grave. As he did this something caught his eye. He picked it up and discreetly placed it inside his pocket. He then picked up a shovel and sprinkled a thin layer of soil on top. The gravediggers would complete the task of refilling the grave with soil once the congregation had left.

It was a time of reflection for Carlos, who in his mind was turning the priceless ring he had just retrieved. This lost ring seemed to represent the circle of life, and Carlos thought it was particularly poignant now that Hugh and Agnes were buried together. He also thought that, if he gave the same amount of devotion to Ana as Hugh had to Agnes, he would have a wonderful married life ahead of him.

Once the burial proceedings had concluded, the weather cleared up and within minutes there was not one cloud in the sky. Carlos and Ana announced their departure before the approaching tide closed off the island.

'Thank you, everybody, for your kindness and hospitality. My wife and I will return soon to see the headstone that I hope Reverend Collins will be able to arrange once we've written to you with a suitable inscription.'

'Yes, it would be my pleasure. We'll look forward to seeing you again soon.'

As they drove across the causeway to return their hire car to an anxiously waiting owner they switched on the car radio.

Epilogue

'Good afternoon. This is a pilot broadcast for the forthcoming BBC Radio Newcastle. In the news today, a memorial service took place on the Holy Island where it is reported a local woman who was falsely convicted of murder was buried together with her husband after more than six hundred years apart. It is also reported that the current family are looking into the possibility of a Royal Prerogative of Mercy. In other news, members of a local astronomy group have indicated recent northern light activity, unusual for the time of year but tonight weather conditions are perfect.'

That night an Aurora Borealis shone above Dunstanburgh Castle that was deemed by some to have been the most wonderful ever seen in living history.

The broadcast had ended and Carlos switched off the radio. He smiled at Ana and she looked back at him and as she did so she felt a tiny twinge in her stomach.

'Could it be?' she thought.

Carlos had noticed that she had stopped drinking in the last couple of days. Neither of them knew it yet, but their unborn daughter, conceived in Northumberland, would have magnificent green eyes. They would name her Agnes and she would wear the recently discovered ring on her wedding day.

The End.

Acknowledgements

THANK you, Chrissie for coming into my life and giving me the inspiration to write the novel. Thanks also to Amy Vinn who designed the beautiful bespoke ring shown below and provided a professional service with an eye for detail. Thanks also to my nephew, William Haslam, for the book-cover design. In addition, Mr David Newton was most helpful for his initial input with the cover http://www.cambridgemashow.com/david-newton/ and his brother Pete provided contact details and general words of wisdom. Thanks to Vicki Burkitt created the beautiful artwork of Mabel on the tribute page and to all those who read the book before launch offering their critiques, including Mr D.Smith, Chrissie, Harriet, Lee and Kath, Tania and Sue to name but a few; my apologies if I have missed anyone out. Finally, my thanks to Hannah Weatherill for editing the novel and for all her advice and to Mrs Kim Bibby-Wilson of the Northumberland Language Society (http://www.northumbriana.org.uk/langsoc/) for her assistance with the ring-inscription wording. Also all the staff at Youcaxton publications, especially Mr Bob Fowke, for all their expert help.

Where possible I have sought permission from businesses mentioned in the novel although all are described in a positive manner. Those who responded include Mr. Neil Robson of L.Robson & Sons Ltd (Craster Kippers). My thanks to the Anna Foster show on Radio BBC Newcastle who contacted me and invited me to discuss things inspired by the north; this was very helpful. http://www.bbc.co.uk/programmes/p02mnny4

Indeed, many news channels that have highlighted the sad state of plastic pollution in the sea and this has motivated me to collect any rubbish I see on the beach; it should not be there in the first place. If we all do our bit we can make the planet a better place for future generations.

Ring designed by Amy Vinn © 2016 Harriet Kelsall Jewellery Design Ltd. All rights reserved.

https://www.hkjewellery.co.uk/

https://www.hkjewellery.co.uk/ring-11627-chrissies-9ct-rose-gold-northumberland-inspired-ring

Tribute to Mabel

2016-2017

SHORTLY before the release of this book Chrissie's beloved spaniel Mabel was tragically run over and killed in the south of England. Mabel will sadly be missed by us both; she brought much enjoyment to our lives. Mabel loved nothing more than chasing a frisbee along the beaches in Northumberland or walking in the woodlands or the Cheviots.

The picture opposite which was kindly painted by a friend is of Mabel proudly wearing a collar designed with the Northumberland flag and encapsulates her energy. She was a dog who gave much affection and was adored by many including my local ramblers group

As with the loss of a loved one whether human or a pet, we have fond memories to hold onto and hope one day that we will be reunited. Mabel's ashes were scattered on the Holy Island which is now her home forever. RIP

Artwork © Vicki Burkitt 2017